HARKLIGHTS

In memory of my father,
your sunshine light lives on.

First published in the UK in 2021 by Usborne Publishing Ltd., Usborne House,
83-85 Saffron Hill, London EC1N 8RT, England. usborne.com
Usborne Verlag, Usborne Publishing Ltd., Prüfeninger Str. 20, 93049 Regensburg,
Deutschland, VK Nr. 17560

Text and illustrations copyright © Tim Tilley, 2021

The right of Tim Tilley to be identified as the author and illustrator of this work has
been asserted by him in accordance with the Copyright, Designs and Patents Act, 1988.

The name Usborne and the Balloon logo are Trade Marks of Usborne Publishing Ltd.

This is a work of fiction. The characters, incidents, and dialogues are products of the
author's imagination and are not to be construed as real. Any resemblance to actual
events or persons, living or dead, is entirely coincidental.

A CIP catalogue record for this book is available from the British Library.

JFM MJJASOND/21 ISBN 9781474966603 05365/1

Printed and bound in Great Britain by CPI Group (UK) Ltd, Croydon, CR0 4YY

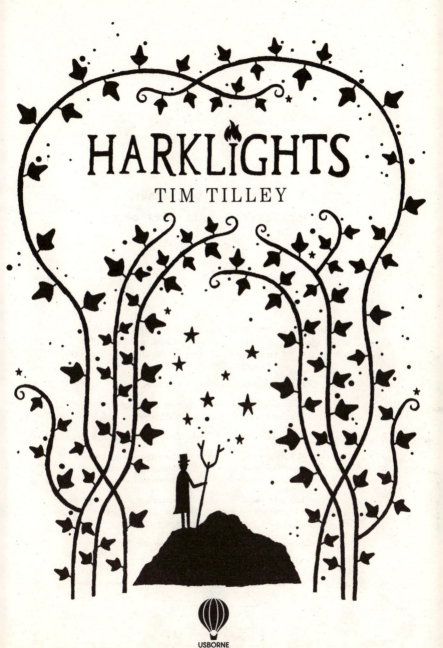

HARKLIGHTS

TIM TILLEY

USBORNE

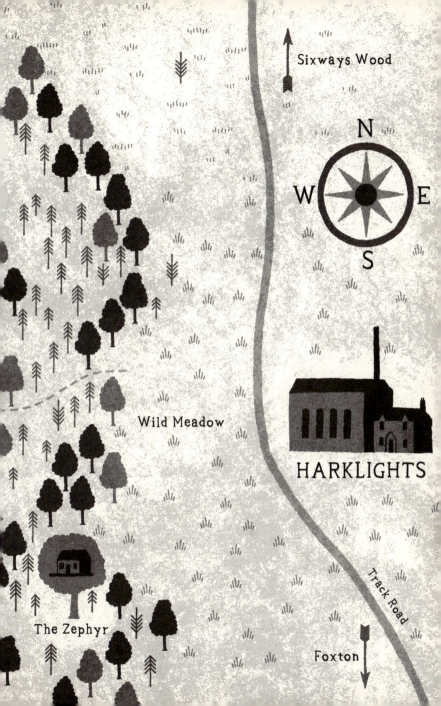

Sixways Wood

N
W   E
S

Wild Meadow

HARKLIGHTS

The Zephyr

Track Road

Foxton

CHAPTER ONE

THE NEW ORPHAN

Old Ma Bogey is coming. We wait, like coiled clock-springs, for announcements. Wait to hear who's getting punishment, or if there's a new orphan. Wingnut jumps out of his seat as Old Ma Bogey marches into the dining room, wearing her usual black fitted jacket and floor-sweeping skirt. Her grey hair is pulled up in a bun at the back of her head. She carries her beating stick. A small boy follows in her wake.

I stop holding my breath and let out a sigh.

It's a new orphan.

The small boy looks terrified. He's already dressed in the grey clothes we all wear. A black-and-yellow box of Harklights Everstrikes rattles in his hand. Old Ma Bogey gives every new orphan a box of matches. She says it's a gift, the first matchbox packed for you.

Most of us orphans call Miss Boggett "Old Ma Bogey" behind her back. We call her this because the first thing she does when a new orphan arrives is to take their name away and give them a new one.

Old Ma Bogey wears an iron thumb-guard, which looks like part of a knight's gauntlet. She wears it all the time, even though it's only to protect her thumb when firing her crossbow.

The matchbox rattles as the boy climbs the steps to the stage.

Old Ma Bogey strikes the stage with the tip of her beating stick and growls, "Stand up straight."

I wonder if the small boy knew his parents. I can't remember mine. Not their faces. Not whether they lived in a town house, shack or anywhere else. My earliest memories are of the factory: prison-high walls, tall iron gates and an enormous chimney, grime-blackened at its tip.

"This is Bottletop. He is going to be staying with us." Old Ma Bogey jabs her beating stick at me. "Wick, I want *you* to show him how we do things round here."

My stomach tenses. This could wind up getting me another beating. As I get up from my bench seat at one of the long tables, Petal nudges my elbow. "Bet he won't last half a day."

"We'll see." I hope she isn't right. Otherwise that'll be three orphans in a row – gone in a flash – and I'll be working next to an empty seat again.

I collect Bottletop. He's about seven or eight years old, at a guess. His skin is pale as paper – it makes him look as if he's been living in a cellar or a coal shed. He's still rattling the matchbox when I find him a place on the bench next to me.

"She took all your things, didn't she?" I whisper.

Bottletop nods.

"She does that with everybody. I'm Wick."

After a few minutes, a door from the kitchen bangs open and Padlock comes through, wheeling a trolley of empty bowls and a brass tea urn. Padlock is the oldest orphan at the factory, and works as Old Ma Bogey's assistant. His stubble is so rough he can strike matches off it. Sometimes he flicks them at us packsmiths. We hate him almost as much as we hate Old Ma Bogey.

He grabs a bowl with one of his thick hands then

turns on the brass tap, letting loose a stream of lumpish bone-coloured liquid.

Bottletop gapes at the filled bowl.

"Porridge," I say. "We get it for every meal. It's not that bad. It doesn't taste of anything, so you can imagine any flavour you like. Make sure you eat it all up or there'll be trouble." I nod towards Padlock, who's putting a drop of liquid from a brown bottle in the middle of every bowl of porridge he hands out. "And that's medicine. She gives it us so we stay healthy."

Old Ma Bogey and Padlock don't have porridge. At the high table, they eat roast chicken, turkey, duck, sausages and bacon, great joints of beef and lamb, and roast potatoes with thick gravy. For pudding, there's new penny buns, apple pie with custard, sponge cake, plum cake, treacle tart and jam tart, and bread-and-butter pudding. They never share their food, or give us leftovers, even though they leave lots.

After dinner, Old Ma Bogey orders me and Bottletop to come to her office, while Padlock marches the rest of the orphans upstairs. She unlocks the door and ushers us through. Inside, the office is as it always is. Neat and ordered. The desk is empty of paperwork. The only things that sit there are the ink-blotter, oil lamp and the drawer she's taken out from the desk. It's filled with all sorts – tools, machine parts, bits of old pocket watches, brass camera lenses and other odds and ends. These are the things she uses to name us.

The bell jar is still there on the mantelpiece next to the mechanical beetles Old Ma Bogey likes making. The beetles are impossible things, things that should only exist in story-papers and people's imaginations. But somehow, she makes them and they chitter and skitter around her office.

Inside the bell jar is a miniature man, no bigger than a couple of matchboxes stood on top of each other, end on end. He's dressed in doll's clothes and rests on a bed of dried moss and leaves. His skin is thick, leathery, like a glove. His eyes are shut.

Bottletop notices him and has the same reaction as every new orphan – disgust and fascination. He shifts on his feet and says nothing as Old Ma Bogey unlocks one of the low cupboards.

"Here, this is yours," she barks as she hands him a thin wool blanket, the same ash-grey as her hair, the same ash-grey as our clothes. The only colour anyone sees at Harklights – apart from bruises – is Old Ma Bogey's blood-red lipstick.

"And this," she says, handing him a stick of white chalk. "You get a piece once every two weeks and Petal will give you newspaper pictures." A smile curls the corner of her mouth. "Use them to remember the things you *miss*."

Bottletop glances at me, bewildered.

I try and give him a reassuring look.

Scratch, Old Ma Bogey's enormous black cat, skulks into the office and springs up onto the desk. Old Ma

Bogey strokes him with her iron-thumbed hand. She's the only one who can touch him without getting ripped to shreds.

"Right, that's it," barks Old Ma Bogey. "You can go."

As me and Bottletop climb the main stairs to bed, I stop halfway up by the framed box filled with butterflies. Next to it is a photograph of a man wearing spectacles with grey hexagonal lenses, and an unhappy-looking girl. "He's not real, you know, the little man in the bell jar. He's made up – like that fairy that sells floating soap flakes or the Drink Imp that sells lemonade."

I show Bottletop the bathroom, then take him to the dormitory. He clutches his blanket and looks around at the bare floorboards, covered in chalk drawings.

"There aren't any beds," I say, pointing to the rows of chalked-out boxes that show where our beds would go. "We sleep on the floor. You get used to it. Like the stink of match mixture."

Petal sits in the only chair we've got in the dormitory. The other orphans lie on their blankets around her. She straightens her back, making herself look even taller, and wraps her blanket around her shoulders. Then she takes out several sheets of *The Empire Times* from her pocket and unfolds them. She's the one who's given the old newspapers to read each week. She lays the pages on the dormitory floor in rows, sharing out the pictures as if they're sweets. Some of us collect pictures of gentle people to be imaginary parents, or find ones that look like the parents who left us. Some draw them in chalk on the dormitory floor and fall asleep in their arms, only to find them turned to dust by morning.

Petal reads by candlelight. "Preparations are under way for The Festival of Empire at The Crystal Palace in London."

"Festival?"

"The Crystal Palace?" come voices from the blankets.

Petal nods. "To celebrate the King's coronation. Can you imagine if we went? It's going to have an electric railway, an imperial choir and replicas of parliament buildings from all across Empire Britannica!"

I try not to look interested at the mention of replicas.

Wingnut stops drawing an eye on the floor with his broken chalk. "We'd never be allowed to go," he says in a flat tone. Wingnut doesn't like make-believe stories. He only believes in what he knows to be true, like the fact that Petal is the best reader, Scratch hunts small creatures and Old Ma Bogey has a short temper.

The younger orphans chatter noisily.

"Shhh," whispers Petal. "Keep your noise down."

We don't want Padlock coming in and telling us off. Or worse, Old Ma Bogey.

The voices fall silent. Wingnut finishes drawing the chalk eye, giving it eyelashes like sun rays.

Petal clears her throat and finishes reading the news. Then she says, "Who's ready for a story?"

There are nods around the dormitory. Everyone settles down under their thin blankets, including Bottletop, who looks better, but still a bit scared. Petal always makes up stories. They allow you to escape. Change the things you can't change. Be somewhere else. Be someone else.

Petal's eyes widen. "Once there was a clockmaker—"

"Did he work on the Great Clock?" whispers one of the orphans. "The one in London that keeps the Empire running like clockwork?"

"No, this was after. The clockmaker made other clocks. But he was lonely and longed for a daughter, so he made a clockwork one."

I'm only half listening, staring out of the window at

the forest beyond the meadow. I'm waiting for everyone to go to sleep. That's when I get the dormitory all to myself.

Petal carries on with the story. The clockmaker dies and there's no one left to wind up his daughter. She's an orphan, then adopted by a horrid guardian who beats her and makes her wash the floors, even though the water makes her rust.

"Is there going to be a prince?" a small voice calls out at one point.

Petal sighs. "Why do fairy tales need princes to be the answer to problems?"

It's dark outside by the time Petal says, "I'll tell you the rest tomorrow night."

A streak of light flashes across the night sky – there for a moment, then gone.

"Falling star!" I say.

"Another orphan finds a home," adds Petal.

The other orphans – except Wingnut – climb out of their blankets and go to the window, whispering excitedly, imagining what it would be like to be adopted or to escape. But the truth is we're going nowhere – we're like the pinned butterflies in the framed box. No one has ever come to Harklights looking to become a guardian. No orphan ever got away. Once Cog tried to sneak out on one of the lorries, but as all the drivers work for Old Ma Bogey, he only got as far as the end of the lane. That's all we see here – steam lorries, horse-drawn wagons, new motor vans. They take away matches, and deliver wood and food. And we get the orphanage inspector once a year. The inspector meets Old Ma Bogey outside the gates and never sets foot in Harklights.

After Petal snuffs out the candle with her fingers, it takes ages for the younger orphans to settle down. I lie there, listening to the sound of their breathing slow and fade, like winding-down clocks.

When everyone is asleep, I get up and creep across to the fireplace that's not been lit in years. I'm careful not to step on the chalk-drawn flowers – things the other orphans miss so much, things I've never seen. On a hidden ledge inside the chimney are the matchstick buildings I've been making in secret for over a year.

I take the new matches I've nicked from the Match Room today and carefully cut off the strike-tops. Then I glue the final pieces of the chimney into place on my latest model.

I've made a dozen or so, all based on places I've seen in newspaper photographs. I make them to keep my wish of finding a new home alive – stop it from fading, help it come true.

I carefully take the completed building and place it on the deep window sill.

I feel a surge of pride as I admire the finished thing, built one pocketful of matches at a time. It's a grand town house. The sort you might find in London. Four storeys, with large windows and steps running up to a smart-looking front door.

The rising moon shines through the model house's back windows, illuminating the inside, making it look as if there are lights on. I imagine the rooms with roaring fires and books and a workshop for making things. And a new family.

I don't want to break the spell, but the light in the little windows fades as the moon –

nearly full – climbs higher, now silvering the tiny rooftop and the newly finished chimney. I hide the model away and climb under my blanket. As I fall asleep, I hold onto the images of who I could become, as tightly as a new orphan holding a box of Everstrikes on their first day.

Old Ma Bogey's gong wakes us at six o'clock. After going to the bathroom, we march downstairs to the dining room. When Padlock arrives with the trolley, Bottletop gives me a look as if to say, *I can't believe we have porridge for dinner* and *breakfast*.

I say, "You'll get used to it."

"Mmm," says Petal. "I'm going to imagine it's chocolate pudding. Then tonight I'm going to have lemon tart."

"Me too," chorus some of the others.

After breakfast, we all follow Old Ma Bogey and Padlock down the corridor. We stop at the emerald-green door that joins the house to the factory. The Machine's roar has already started. The clanking and clanging is so loud you couldn't hear your own voice even if you dared to speak.

Old Ma Bogey fiddles with a bunch of keys, then unlocks the door and opens it. Beyond it is a set of metal stairs that runs up to the Machine on the first floor. No orphan is ever allowed to set foot on the stairs, except Padlock. Not even the first step.

"Take these sacks of red phosphorus to the cauldron," she says to Padlock. "And make sure there's enough glue."

The waiting sacks look heavy. Padlock shoulders one of them easily and climbs up the stairs. Old Ma Bogey leads us down a winding corridor to another green door. A sign reads:

Inside, a waterfall of matches tumbles down from a ledge at the top of the far wall. Below the waterfall, a conveyor belt runs the length of the room, carrying them away in a river, which then cascades into a massive heap. At regular intervals on either side of the conveyor belt are packsmith workstations, each with two seats and piles of empty matchboxes.

"So, this is where we work," I say to Bottletop as we file in and I lead him to one of the workstations. "The factory has the Machine to make matches, but it still needs us to fill the matchboxes and pack them into crates."

Bottletop nods sadly and mumbles something about wanting soldiers.

"What's that?"

"She took my tin soldiers."

"I'm sorry."

I can't remember if I arrived with any toys, but I've seen pictures of them in the newspapers. It must be sad to have something so special taken away.

I show Bottletop how to take a clutch of matches – not too many, not too few – and sort and pack them into an empty matchbox, then stack them into one of the crates for transporting.

He's useless.

His hands keep jolting as he tries to fill the matchboxes. The matches go everywhere.

I want him to be better than the last orphan I was paired with, but he's even worse.

Maybe Petal's right.

Maybe he won't last half a day.

CHAPTER TWO

THE BOTTOMLESS WELL

After half an hour, Bottletop's nerves calm down a bit. He's still dropping matches though and has only managed around fifty filled matchboxes. I don't have the heart to tell him he's supposed to work at a rate of three hundred an hour. I'm not the fastest packsmith in the factory – that's Wingnut – but I can easily clock over three hundred and sixty an hour on a good day.

I check to see if Padlock is lost in his newspaper. He is. He reads it to make himself look important. All I can see of him are his thick fingers.

I grab a handful of matches. Then I take the penknife that Flint stole from Old Ma Bogey's office and cut off the strike-tops. I paint them with glue from the pot that we use on Sundays, when the Machine is off and we spend all day making the matchboxes for the following week.

Bottletop throws me a look.

"Don't worry about me, you get on with filling your boxes."

Ten minutes later, after the glue has dried, I tap Bottletop's shoulder. "This is for you."

He looks at the little matchstick figure.

"I know it doesn't look much like a soldier…"

Bottletop takes it. He turns it around. A huge smile spreads across his face. "Thanks."

I nod. "You'd better hide it."

As we pack to the grinding rhythm of the Machine, I imagine all the places across Empire Britannica that the matchboxes will end up. The smokestack cities: Manchester, Liverpool, London. Or faraway places, travelling by pocket and steamship, India – where Petal's mother was from – or Africa. I also imagine all the different things they will be used to light. Gaslights, oil lamps, carriage candles.

At eleven o'clock, the Machine is switched off and

the waterfall of matches stops. Padlock puts down his newspaper and shoots dark looks around the room. When I think he's not looking, I slide a pile of matchboxes across to Bottletop's side of the crate.

"Inspection time," I mutter.

Bottletop tenses, his hands clenched tight by his sides. He reminds me of myself when I was younger – I struggled too. Back then, I wished someone would help me. Then Petal arrived and she did.

"I've packed enough matchboxes for the both of us," I whisper. "Trust me. It'll be fine."

But inside, I feel a prickle of doubt. What if Padlock did see me?

Old Ma Bogey appears at the green door.

As everyone stands and turns to look at her, I glance to the pile of matchboxes on Bottletop's side of the crate. I might not be able to change my past, but hopefully I can save Bottletop from a few beatings. Give him better days.

Old Ma Bogey slowly paces between the packsmith workstations. Padlock shadows her like a bodyguard.

She stops by Wingnut and picks up one box between finger and iron thumb, then shakes it and listens to its woody rattle.

"Needs a few more," she barks. With a swift blow, she cuffs Wingnut on the back of his head, knocking the stick of chalk he keeps behind his ear to the floor. "You may be fast, but you also need to be accurate."

I wince. I know the sharp pain of the iron thumb. All of us packsmiths do.

When Old Ma Bogey arrives next to our workstation, Bottletop's shakes have returned.

I hold my breath, waiting for Padlock to say something, but he just scowls.

Old Ma Bogey lifts out a black-and-yellow matchbox from Bottletop's side of the crate and rattles it. "Very good." Then she opens it and checks the red strike-tips are all facing the same way. "You're getting the hang of this."

After putting the matchbox back, her fingers curl like a dying spider, then point. "What is that?"

Bottletop freezes as Old Ma Bogey picks up the matchstick figure he left on the countertop. "It's, it's—"

"We are NOT here to make toys!" she cries, spraying little flecks of spit over the small boy's face. "What do you think this place is – Saint Nicholas's workshop?"

Bottletop is too frightened to say anything.

We both watch as she crushes the little wooden figure in her hand and lets the pieces drop from her fingers like fallen leaves.

"I made it, Miss Boggett," I say in a quiet voice.

"What was that?" Old Ma Bogey's eyes glow with fury. She pinches my ear. "I did not hear you."

The cold of her iron thumb pinches harder and harder, lancing my ear with hot pain as she lifts me off my seat. "I said, I made it."

Old Ma Bogey lets go of my ear. It throbs as if a new heart beats there. "Go to the yard and wait by the wall. Now!"

I leave the Packing Room quickly, clutching my ear, ignoring the horrified faces of Petal and the other packsmith orphans. Old Ma Bogey sending me outside can mean only one thing – the Bottomless Well. The place where orphans go and don't come back.

I step outside onto the bare earth of the yard and stand by the factory wall. My stomach churns. I can't look at the Well. I glance up at the hanging crane claw that unloads the logs from the trucks and drops them down a hatch to feed the Machine. Then I focus on a tiny plant growing out of the brickwork. Thread-like stem.

Two bright green leaves. It's not much more than a seedling, but I didn't think anything ever grew in the yard. The gnarled old tree that stands in the middle never has any leaves. I'm sure the apples we get on our days off twice a year don't come from it.

When the Machine starts up again, marking the end of the inspection, the seedling quivers slightly. I press my hand against the wall and close my eyes, feel the steady tremble of the engine in my bones.

When I open my eyes again, I glimpse a flash of magpie wings out of the corner of my eye, rising up into the air. Then there's a noise, of something light and small dropping to the ground.

A bird in the yard means good luck. I look around and skyward, but it's gone. Then I catch sight of what looks like an acorn beneath the old tree.

I walk over. As I pick it up, I realize it's not a real acorn, it's a wooden cradle with a hood, carved and polished to *look* just like an acorn.

Inside is a tiny woollen blanket, I imagine for a tiny doll. Then the wool moves. I hold my breath, and the world shifts slightly. Underneath is a *baby*, about as long as half a match, with nut-brown eyes and coal-black hair, wriggling away.

For a few moments, I just stare, filled with wonder.

I can't believe my eyes.

I hold the acorn-cradle close to my face and watch the smiling baby happily kicking its feet in the air and waving its plump fists. "Impossible," I mutter. "No one can make a clockwork toy with parts so small..."

The words catch like a bone in my throat.

It's not an automaton.

It's real.

A real tiny baby wearing a moss nappy.

I glance from my palm to the cracked wall that circles the Bottomless Well. I'm crying on the inside, unseen tears. The baby has been abandoned at Harklights, just like I was.

I want to tell the baby that everything is going to be alright. But I can't be sure.

And now I hear a familiar noise coming from the factory.

Whack.

Whack.

Whack.

Old Ma Bogey's beating stick. It sounds as if she's practising her strikes as she makes her way down the hall. Maybe she won't throw me down the Well. Maybe she'll just thrash me to within half an inch of my life.

I carefully hide the acorn-cradle in my shirt pocket where I keep my piece of chalk.

As I see Old Ma Bogey emerging from the shadows of the porch, my heart turns to lead. She's pulling a handcart piled high with every single one of my matchbox buildings: town houses and tower-houses, grand mansions and hotels.

How did she find out about them? Padlock didn't know. And if the other orphans had seen me, they would never snitch. Our rule is to never tell on anyone.

"It seems you have been busy apart from packing matches." Old Ma Bogey's voice is soft, almost warm, before it turns cold. "Petal told me."

Petal.

I can't believe it. I *won't* believe it. We're friends. She helped cover my quota for months. She comforted me when Flint went down the Well, gave me the last sweet she had been saving. And we swore a secret oath together: *Never tell Old Ma Bogey anything, never come back if you get a new home, and never forget our friendship.*

Old Ma Bogey must be lying.

"She told me all about your secret models."

"Petal would never—"

"Well, it was *one* of your orphan friends. Give me the penknife and glue pot."

I take them from my trouser pocket and hand them to her, trying not to let my fingers tremble. "I'm sorry."

"Oh, you're sorry now. Everybody is sorry when they get caught. All this time, you've been *stealing* from me." Old Ma Bogey screws her lips up tight. "I don't think a beating will get through to you." She lifts something up that was hidden behind the models.

A paraffin can.

"Oh, please," I cry, "don't burn them! I'll pack more matchboxes than ever..."

She unscrews the cap and pours.

Glug.

Glug.

Glug.

All over my precious buildings.

"I *know* you will," she says with a horrid grin. Then she strikes a match and tosses it onto the models.

"Matches are meant to burn. It's what they are made for," growls Old Ma Bogey. "Stay here. Watch your models turn to ashes and think about what you've done. Then back to work."

I nod in a daze as the stack of miniature buildings is engulfed in flames. The walls click and hiss as they burn and cave in on themselves – till all that remains is a mass of glowing embers, crooked matches sticking out like the ribs of a blackened skeleton.

I wonder if I'll ever leave and find a new home, wonder if I'll ever get to make another model again. I touch the shirt pocket over my heart. At least I kept the acorn baby safe.

I want to show Petal. She'll be able to help me, but it'll need to be away from the others. I know Petal would never snitch on me. Old Ma Bogey is only saying it because she knows we are friends. She's trying to take away one of the few things I have left.

As I cross the yard, I notice Scratch's bowl in the shade of the porch, filled with milk.

I know from my bits of newspaper education that babies drink milk. When I take the acorn-cradle out of my pocket, the baby smiles at me with bright eyes.

"You hungry?" I whisper.

I tear off a tiny strip of fabric from my shirt and dip it into Scratch's bowl. Once soaked, I hold the strip close to the baby. Whether it's curiosity or instinct I don't know, but the baby holds the tiny strip and suckles. Once

it's finished, I carefully place the acorn-cradle back in my pocket. Then I lift up Scratch's bowl and drink, forcing myself to stop before I finish it.

The afternoon shift passes slowly. I pack matchboxes, trying not to remember my models going up in flames, wondering if any of the other orphans did snitch on me. Every time I glance over, each looks guilt-free. Somehow, I get the feeling it wasn't any of them.

My mind whirrs with thoughts of what would happen if Old Ma Bogey got hold of the baby. Would she put it in a bell jar like the miniature man? I tell myself she would put it in a cage so people from miles and miles around could buy tickets to come and look at it. In place of matches, packsmiths would put miniature acorn-baby dolls into matchboxes to be sold as souvenirs. Outside, excited crowds would line up and Old Ma Bogey's rough voice would boom through a brass loudhailer: "Roll up! Roll up! Come and see the Smallest Baby in the World!"

At the end of the shift, when the Machine's noise dies down, I thank the stars the acorn baby isn't crying.

"You alright?" asks Petal, as we file out of the door into the corridor. "Did she threaten to throw you down the Well?"

"Not this time."

"That's a twist of luck." Her face is innocent with bright eyes.

I wait till the other packsmiths pass and we're alone in the corridor. "I found something. Something incredible. Like in your stories—"

"Wick, what do you mean?"

I grab Petal's arm. "Your stories – the ones where things happen that change everything. But I can't show you here. We need to keep it secret from the others."

Petal shrugs off my grip. "Okay, I'll tell Padlock you don't feel too well and I'm taking you up to bed. Wait here a moment."

A smile lurks at the corner of her mouth when she returns. "Padlock says Old Ma Bogey doesn't like anyone missing dinner. You'll get two bowls of porridge for breakfast."

I cover my mouth and pretend to be sick.

I lead Petal up to the bathroom and open the door. She follows me inside.

"What did you find, another stag beetle?"

I take the acorn-cradle from my pocket. The baby is awake, looking up at us with wonder.

Petal gasps and her eyes light up. "Is it real?"

I nod.

"Can I hold it?"

Carefully I pass the acorn-cradle into her waiting hands. She holds the cradle close, eyes sparkling with tears. "I always believed in impossible things," she whispers.

It's true, she's always believed in magic.

When she passes the cradle back, there's a smell coming from the moss nappy. I open it and there's a slick of greenish poo everywhere.

Petal wrinkles her nose and steps away. "Urgh, that's disgusting."

"Blimey, look at all this muck," I say. "Let's get you sorted out."

I run the tap till there's a shallow pool in the bottom of the sink, gently lie the baby in it and wash the poo off. There's no way I can make a nappy, so instead I wrap her in another strip from my shirt and tie it carefully. "That'll keep you clean till tomorrow."

Now the acorn baby has a new nappy, Petal comes close again. "Has she been fed?"

"I gave her some of Scratch's milk from the porch. I don't know how we're going to get more though."

Petal's eyes twinkle. "Don't worry, I'll think of something... And how about a tiny bottle? I'm sure there's one in the naming drawer."

I can't imagine how we're going to get in Old Ma Bogey's office and then sneak out to the yard for more milk without anyone finding out. But together, our chances seem better. I tell her about the matchstick models and one of the orphans snitching to Old Ma Bogey.

"I don't know who it could be," says Petal in disbelief. "But I won't say anything about the baby." She mimes locking her lips and throwing away the key. "I better get back down to dinner or Padlock will come looking for me."

As I head into the empty dormitory, and cross to my place by the wall, I hope Petal and I can keep the baby safe. I ask myself where she's going to sleep.

Maybe I can make a new matchstick house...

CHAPTER THREE

THE MIDNIGHT FOLK

I must have fallen asleep, as the next thing I know I wake to darkness. I'm still curled on my side with my back to everyone. I find the acorn-cradle is still there, cupped in my hand. Moonlight floods into the dormitory through the curtainless windows and pools on the bare floorboards. From down in the hall comes the steady stirring chimes of the grandfather clock. I count each of them. It's midnight.

I wait a few moments to make sure everyone is fast asleep, then peer at the tiny cradle again. The baby is sleeping too. I'm wondering how Petal and I are going to get her more of Scratch's milk, when there's a light tapping on the window.

I freeze.

Slowly I close my hand over the acorn-cradle.

I look up and the hairs rise on the back of my neck. There, at the window, is a little man silhouetted against the moonlight, wearing a hat and cloak. For a horrible moment, I think he's the little man from the bell jar come back from the dead. But then, with a rush of excitement, I realize who he is. He must be another one, a live one! What if he's the acorn baby's father? This is a first. No parent has ever changed their mind and come back to the orphanage.

"You came back for her," I whisper into the night.

I want to jump up and race to the window, but I move cautiously, quietly. When I reach the window, I see there's a little woman and a girl there too, dressed in coats and boots.

I open up the window, grinning in awe, and let the little people climb through onto the window sill. Here, in the milk-blue light, I can see the girl isn't much younger than me, and they all have the same dark hair as the acorn baby.

"You're her parents, aren't you?" I whisper.

The little man steps forward. "Genna here is her mother," he says in a gentle earthy voice, pointing to the kind-faced little woman with short hair. "An' we are her friends. I'm Papa Herne an' this is Nissa, my daughter."

The girl has a wild tangle of hair, swept back from her face. She adjusts a tiny catapult that's tucked into her belt and raises a hand in greeting.

"I'm Wick," I mumble, hardly believing this is happening. "It's good to see you."

I put the acorn-cradle down. As Genna picks her baby up, she wakes up and smiles.

"Thank you for keeping her safe," says Papa Herne. "Genna would thank you herself, but she don't talk."

Genna looks up at me with a fragile grin. I wonder if something bad happened to her. There are several orphans at Harklights who never say anything.

"We saw you outside from the wall when you found

the baby," continues Papa Herne. "But then yer mother came along."

"She's not my mother," I say.

"Well, as a thank you, can we be of any assistance to you in yer home?"

"This isn't my home – it's an orphanage."

Papa Herne blinks and rubs his smooth chin. He looks as if he doesn't know whether an orphanage is a good or a bad thing.

Nissa looks me up and down. "Where's yer home if it isn't here?"

"I've not got one. That's what an orphanage is for. It's a place for abandoned children." I glance at Genna. "I thought you'd left your baby here."

The little people's eyes grow wide in horror.

"No," says Papa Herne. "She weren't abandoned. Hobs would never do that. A magpie stole the cradle an' then…"

"What's a Hob?" I ask.

"It's what we are – little folk. We're like humans, only we got more forest in our hearts." Papa Herne's words die off as he looks around at the orphans sleeping on the wooden floor. Then he fixes his eyes on me. "Well, we need to repay yer kindness in looking after Tiya—"

43

"Can he come live with us?" says Nissa.

Papa Herne raises his eyebrows and looks thoughtful. "That's exactly what I were thinking," he says with a smile.

There's a strange stirring in my chest as I hear the words "come live with us". I push the feeling down. I don't want to get my hopes up, in case they don't mean it. "You wouldn't want me. I reckon I'd just get in your way. I'm too big."

"Havenwood Forest is home to all sizes," says Papa Herne with warmth in his voice.

"It's true," says Nissa.

I glance at the Hobs. A mother, a father, two daughters. The shape of a family. It's all I've ever wanted. And this might be the only chance I'll get. Something Petal said about opportunities comes back to me: *Take them if you find them.*

I creep over to Petal and tap her shoulder. She wakes quietly. Her eyes widen when she sees the Hobs on the window sill.

"This is Petal," I say, bringing her over to meet them. "She helped. Can she come with us?"

"Of course," says Papa Herne.

Nissa grins and presses her hands together.

"Go where?" says Petal.

"New home," I whisper. I can hardly believe I'm saying the words. "We're getting out of here."

Petal hesitates, her eyes gleaming. "What about the others? Can they come too?"

I glance back at the rest of the packsmiths, some asleep in the arms of chalk-drawn parents. I feel a pang of guilt about leaving them.

Papa Herne scratches his head. "I'd like to take them all with us, but what about that lady? The one who's not yer mother. Would she let them go? I don't think we could get them all out without her noticing."

"No," I say sharply. "And if she caught us, everyone would be punished."

Petal glances back at the other orphans too. "It would be too risky…"

"This could be it," I say. "Our only chance."

Petal nods, then takes a breath and holds it. "Alright, yes."

Papa Herne smiles up at me and Petal. "That's settled. I don't think our leaf-rope will hold yer weight. Have you got something stronger?"

A bone-deep fear grips me when I think how far it might be to the ground – how far I would fall if I slipped. "I'm not…I can't climb."

"We can use the stairs," says Petal.

"Alright," says Papa Herne. "We'll meet you outside by that old tree." I must look worried, scared or both, because he adds, "Don't worry, you won't have to climb over the wall."

Petal and I know where all the creak points are on the main stairs. Flint taught us before he got kicked down the Bottomless Well for hiding Old Ma Bogey's iron thumb. A wave of excitement runs through me as we creep downstairs, stepping through moonlight and shadow.

I can't believe we're going to escape.

Never come back if you get a new home.

That's part of our secret oath. I never dared hope we'd find a new home together.

I wonder if the Hobs know of a secret tunnel that goes under the yard wall. Or maybe there's a secret door, like in Petal's stories.

Creeak.

I wince as the stair tread groans under my foot.

"Watch where you step," whispers Petal. "Don't make another noise or we might get caught."

It's not that easy. The problem with creak points is once you step on them—

Creeak.

—there's no going back. Not without making another sound.

Petal and I wait, listening to the grandfather clock tick-tocking away each moment.

No one comes for us.

We take our time on the next steps, tiptoeing slowly.

At the bottom of the stairs, we put our boots on and step onto the tiles of the hall floor. We cross over to Old Ma Bogey's drawing room, where she sleeps in a high-backed chair. We need to find the keys for the front door. Of course, it's locked. And there's not one or two locks, there's twenty-six. That's twenty-six different keys.

The drawing-room door is ajar. Taking a deep breath, I gently push it open. I've never been in before. The contents of the room are edged with orange light from the dying fire ticking in the grate. Old Ma Bogey's high-backed armchair looms next to an enormous fireplace.

We sneak across the half-lit drawing room, passing a gramophone and a large cabinet with wire mesh panels. Old Ma Bogey is fast asleep, sitting upright. Her grey hair is still scraped into a tight bun, but instead of a jacket she wears a housecoat. Scratch is asleep on her lap.

Petal and I can't help but look at her right hand. She's still wearing her iron thumb.

We go back to hunting for the keys. Petal searches the large cabinet, while I search the table next to Old Ma Bogey's chair. There's a collection of *Machinarium* journals and a bottle of sleep tincture.

The bunch of keys isn't here. But I have a good idea where they'll be.

I hold my breath and slip a hand into one of Old Ma Bogey's pockets.

She stirs and twists in her seat.

We freeze.

Scratch jumps off her lap and slips into the shadows.

For a moment, I think Old Ma Bogey's going to wake up and grab my hand, but she sighs and her steady breathing continues. With quiet relief, I pull my hand out and try the other pocket. The keys aren't there either. There's only a handful of silver crowns and sixpence coins, a sweet covered in fluff, and some hairpins.

We carry on searching the room. Petal looks through a small bookcase. Mounted on the wall above it is Old Ma Bogey's crossbow. Alongside it, over the fireplace, rests her prized double-barrelled shotgun. The one she cleans and oils and uses to shoot the birds that land in the yard and on the roof. I creep across the room to search the mantelpiece. But before I reach it, I step on something soft.

There's an almighty yowl and I realize the black shape I've trodden on is Scratch.

Old Ma Bogey wakes in an instant. Her cold grey eyes fix on me, then Petal. "WHAT DO YOU THINK YOU'RE DOING?" she roars.

We bolt for the door, glancing back to see Old Ma Bogey out of her chair. I pull back the curtains from the two window sills flanking the front door, frantically searching for the keys. They're not there.

"NO ONE gets away from me!" snarls Old Ma Bogey. She appears in the doorway of her drawing room and raises her shotgun.

We duck.

There's a deafening crack. One of the side windows explodes behind me.

Without thinking, I yank the curtain from its rail to cover the jagged edges, then launch myself through the broken glass. Petal tumbles through after me.

We land uncut on the bare earth outside, get to our feet quickly and run. The Hobs are past the tree, more than halfway across the moonlit yard. They look frozen in shock. The acorn baby bawls at the top of her lungs. I don't think they've heard a shotgun firing before.

I put Old Ma Bogey's bad shot down to the fact she's just woken up. Next time we won't be so lucky.

"Run for your lives!" I shout.

"She's coming!" cries Petal.

The Hobs snap out of their daze and scurry towards the wrought-iron gates, slipping through the bars.

I try to pull them open, but they're locked. The gates are always locked, unless there's a delivery.

Another crack.

Buckshot explodes by my feet, ripping up a spray of dusty soil.

Petal and I panic. We run to the one place that can shield us from Old Ma Bogey's gun – the gnarled old tree.

"Come out, you little toerags!" screeches Old Ma Bogey. "I know you're there."

I chance a quick glance to see where Old Ma Bogey is, but she fires again. Buckshot whistles past my ear.

I glance over to the Hobs, who are waiting on the other side of the gates. Papa Herne stands next to his daughter and Genna, who's calming her baby. They glance at each other as if they can't make up their minds whether to wait for us or leave.

"Don't go," I mumble in a quiet voice. I feel the hope of a new home fading. Maybe they didn't really mean it when they said we could live with them.

I look up at the gnarled tree, which is bent over like a broken-backed man. It's an easy climb – if I was any good – but there's no way its branches can offer us any shelter. If Old Ma Bogey can pick pigeons off her roof, then she could easily shoot us out of a tree.

I look back to the gates. The Hobs are gone.

"No," sobs Petal.

My heart shrinks. I feel crushed, but I'm not surprised they left. No one from Harklights ever found a new home before, so why did I think we'd be any different?

There's the sound of more breaking glass.

I chance another look.

Old Ma Bogey smashes the jagged shards with the butt of her shotgun. Then she climbs through the window and marches across the yard. Her iron thumb pushes more cartridges into the loading chamber. I've never seen her so full of fury. It won't take long for her to either grab us or shoot us. We only have the gnarled tree to run around and no other place to hide.

As she draws close, a trembling starts in my legs. Petal squeezes my hand. I press my back against the ragged bark. This can only go two ways. Wait to be caught or give ourselves up.

Just as I'm about to step out with my hands raised, the tree creaks and groans. It sounds like it's going to fall. I wonder if it's going to land on Old Ma Bogey and pin her to the ground.

I crouch down and stare up in awe. The tree is wreathed in a wash of dancing green light, shot through with greenish white sparks, like the Northern Lights have got snagged in the branches. A trail of this extraordinary light twists all the way to the main gates. Papa Herne stands there, holding a twig tipped with light.

I gaze at him, open-mouthed.

"Magic," says Petal, her voice full of brightness.

I never believed in it. Not like Petal. I thought it was all conjuring tricks and fairy stories used to sell things. But it's real – it's happening right now.

The gnarled tree shudders and trembles. It doesn't fall. Instead it's twisting, transforming. The bent-over trunk thickens and two prong-like branches grow lower until they touch the bare earth and shape into hooves.

Petal and I watch, transfixed.

The roots at the tree's base writhe up and twist into another set of hooves, while the loftier branches become a rack of antlers. It's turning into a creature of twisted roots and bark and branches.

When fully-formed, the tree-stag creaks and raises his wooden head, just as Old Ma Bogey raises her double-barrelled shotgun.

CHAPTER FOUR

OAKHOME

We brace ourselves behind the tree-stag, but I know we're a clear shot for Old Ma Bogey now. I squeeze my eyes shut, waiting for her to bark a command or shoot.

Hooves drum the bare earth like a beating heart.

I flick my eyes open to see the tree-stag bravely charging Old Ma Bogey. She stays rooted to the spot, the barrels of her gun gleaming in the moonlight.

In a flash, the tree-stag ploughs into her, knocking her shotgun from her hand. She falls to the ground, her scream echoing around Harklights' walls. Packsmith faces appear at the dormitory window. Lamplight shines from Padlock's room.

In the yard, the tree-stag circles and charges towards us.

We stand aside so he can pass by freely, but he stops

and kneels down, lowering his crown of antlers, willing us to climb onto his powerful back.

Petal climbs up easily and reaches down a hand. "Wick, get on—"

My feet don't move. Fear shoots through me.

"I can't," I struggle to say. "I've never been any good with heights."

"It's not that high."

I know she's right, but it doesn't make any difference. All I can think about is the Bottomless Well. Standing by the dizzying edge. What a long way down it is.

Petal tries to pull me up, but it's as if my feet are made of lead. As she jumps down, Padlock appears in the yard. He races over to where Old Ma Bogey lies.

"Quick!" cries Petal.

Somehow, with her help, I clamber onto the tree-stag's back. Once I've found a good grip on his mane, the tree-stag charges off – without Petal.

Maybe he doesn't realize she's been left behind.

"No, wait!" I cry, holding on tightly. I don't know how to make the tree-stag stop. I clamp my legs to his sides as I'm thrown back and forth. I try digging in my heels but it doesn't work. "We need to get Petal!"

As the tree-stag circles the yard, Old Ma Bogey grabs her shotgun again and lifts it awkwardly where she lies. Then she unleashes a shot.

BANG.

I flinch.

The shot narrowly misses me and hits one of the tree-stag's antlers, blasting part of it away.

The tree-stag doesn't slow – instead, he gallops faster.

I squeeze my eyes shut and concentrate on not falling off. When I open my eyes again, we're set on a collision course with the yard wall. I brace myself and grip tighter.

Out of the corner of my eye, I see Padlock grab Petal's arm. She twists and turns, trying to pull away. "Let go of me!"

I feel torn inside. I want to help, but I can't. There's no way the tree-stag is stopping. I wonder if he's going to try and crash through the wall, but then he springs into the air, leaping impossibly high. We go up, up, up and over.

We land on the other side of the wall with a crash of hooves and a spray of dry soil. We're on an empty dirt track. Beyond, in all directions, is moonlit meadowland

– rising and falling and stretching as far as the eye can see. It's the first time I've ever seen outside the orphanage. I've always known it's in the middle of nowhere – a forgotten corner at the edge of Empire, but I never realized there was so much open space.

I feel a burst of excitement. *We made it.* But it quickly fades.

My heart sinks.

Petal didn't make it.

I look up at the wall etched in moonlight, then at Papa Herne, who's standing on the track with Nissa and Genna. "We need to go back for Petal."

On the other side of the gates, Old Ma Bogey is back on her feet, raging obscenities about her injured left hand.

"I'm sorry," Papa Herne says. "Our wild magic can only transform nature. It won't do a thing on a brick wall or those cold-iron gates. They're man-made. Yer lucky you had a tree in the yard before, but there's nothing there I can use now to help her."

Petal is still struggling to get free from Padlock. "Wick!" she cries. "Get away before she catches you!"

"I can't leave you," I cry out.

"One of us should get away!"

"Padlock – open the gates!" barks Old Ma Bogey. She grabs Petal's hand, squeezing it with her iron thumb.

"Quick," cries Petal. "You have to go for the both of us!"

My stomach tightens. To escape and leave your friend feels worse than trying to escape and getting caught. It's the sort of punishment Old Ma Bogey would come up with.

The bunch of keys rattles wildly as Padlock searches for the right one.

"I don't think we should hang around," says Papa Herne. He looks up at the tree-stag and makes a clicking sound with his tongue. "Come on, we must go."

"We can't go..." I start to say, but my words trail off.

The little man in the bell jar on the mantelpiece in Old Ma Bogey's office was definitely a Hob. I picture a row of bell jars filled with my new friends.

Padlock is still rattling the gate keys as the tree-stag lowers his head and the Hobs climb up into his rack of antlers.

"Get them! Don't let them get away!" barks Old Ma Bogey, as she drags Petal across the yard.

The Hobs wind leaf-rope around themselves and the antler prongs, strapping themselves and the acorn baby in.

My heart almost breaks at leaving Petal behind. "I'll never forget you!"

"I'll never forget you too!" she yells, as she's dragged into the darkness of the house.

The tree-stag straightens his neck and crosses the lane to the meadow before breaking into a canter, then a gallop. I grip onto the bark tufts of his mane like before. We race through the moonlit sea of wild grass. Despite my sorrow, the rush of cold air is exhilarating. I breathe in deep and it's as if I'm breathing for the first time. I look to the Hobs strapped to the tree-stag's antlers, then glance back across the silver-blue meadow.

Blazing stars glisten and wink overhead. I can't believe this is happening, that I'm finally away from Harklights – that I'm riding on the back of some kind of magical tree-creature.

I grip the tree-stag's bark mane tighter.

Magic is real.

Behind us, Harklights keeps shrinking.

My stomach tightens again. I feel awful that Petal got caught. If I'd been able to climb onto the tree-stag, we'd have both got away, and we'd be escaping together. "I'll come back," I murmur, "and rescue you."

I turn and look ahead, along with the Hobs. I wonder where they're taking me and what their home is like. Do they live in treehouses? Or something like my matchstick buildings?

The dark shape of the forest looms closer on the horizon, an ever-rising wall of trees.

The tree-stag slows to a trot. As we enter the forest, the acorn baby is asleep again. The trees are massive, rising higher than the Harklights factory, and there are more than I can count. Ancient trees with gnarled bark and widespread leafless branches. Towering pines that are sentries over the forest. Petal would like it here.

She always liked stories with forests in them.

We ride for a long time in silence, listening to the night-time sounds. In the moonlight, Papa Herne points out a hedgehog – something I've only seen in newspaper pictures. An owl hoots. It's followed by a screech-cry that turns my blood cold. I clutch the tree-stag's mane more tightly.

"Foxes," whispers Papa Herne. "Up to their crafty ways."

Nights at Harklights are quiet. After the Machine is switched off at six o'clock, the only sound is the grandfather clock in the hall. But out here, the forest's silence keeps breaking. I wonder how the Hobs are able to sleep.

I take a deep breath, filling my lungs again with fresh air and the smell of what must be earth and leaves.

"What's the tree-stag's name?" I ask Papa Herne.

"He don't have one. You should call him something."

"He should be called Half Crown. Petal always said finding them was lucky."

Papa Herne nods. "Half Crown it is then."

The tree-stag's wooden ears tip back as if he approves.

Some way ahead of us, small pinpricks of light appear, like a secret cluster of stars in the forest.

As we draw closer, I realize the lights are coming from tiny rounded windows set into huts built of twigs and sticks, moss and leaves. Each hut looks like two bird nests on top of each other, one upturned. Most of the huts nestle at the foot of several mighty trees in a circular clearing, but some of them perch on low branches. There's a small fire in the centre. A Hob woman and man sit by it, their faces lit by firelight, like newspaper pictures yellowed by the sun. By their wide-eyed surprise, I guess they don't see big people very much.

"Here we are," says Papa Herne. "This is Oakhome. Wick, I'd like you to meet Mama Herne an' Finn, Tiya's father."

"We were so worried," says Mama Herne, getting up as we approach. She looks motherly and kind.

"Mama," cries Nissa, "look what we brought back!"

Mama Herne peers up at me and smiles. "Pleased to meet you."

"Thank the forest you found Tiya," says Finn, standing too.

"She were taken inside a human building," Papa Herne continues. "Wick looked after her, kept her safe."

Genna hands the acorn baby to Finn. My heart hurts as they hug. I want to know what it's like to belong and be loved.

Finn's voice wavers. "Thank you."

"I was happy to help," I reply as Half Crown kneels down and I climb off, relieved to be back on the ground.

Papa Herne, Nissa and Mama Herne talk quietly. Mama Herne glances over at me with a sad look. I guess he's telling her about how I was abandoned.

I walk over to get a closer look at one of the nest-homes. It's made of twigs and moss and feathers woven tightly together. I can't tell if it's been glued. I kneel down and peer through the window into a single room. Next to a nest-bed is a polished miniature table, a stack of different-sized acorn bowls and a tiny jar somehow filled with fireflies. On the floor is a miniature carpet runner, which I realize was once a tapestry bookmark. Above the bed hangs a halfpenny stamp of the old king.

"Where's he gonna sleep?" I catch Mama Herne saying.

I rub the back of my neck, feeling awkward, like a new orphan. I wonder if Papa Herne and Nissa were too quick to invite me and Petal to live with them, that they didn't think it through. And now, here in the forest, it's clear things aren't going to work out.

This is what a home looks like, I think, looking at the huts.

"He can sleep here by the fire for tonight," says Papa Herne.

Mama Herne smiles and touches her lips. "Yeah… there's that blanket. It's mostly all there."

"I'll go get it," says Papa Herne. "An' lots of leaves from the underground store."

"I'll come along too!" cries Nissa.

They climb again onto Half Crown's head. Papa Herne makes a clucking sound with his tongue.

I watch them leave the circle of firelight and pass into moonlight, turning the colour of cold stone.

"Come, sit yerself down," says Mama Herne, patting the leaves next to her. There's a Hob-sized book by her feet. Its pages are filled with tiny handwriting.

I sit carefully, so there's no danger I'll break anything. It feels strange to be by a fire, next to the tree-homes, when my model homes burned only hours ago.

"I can read," I say, peering closer at the tiny book. "I learned at Harklights. Ratchet taught us in secret at the end of our shifts. It was three years before Old Ma Bogey found out."

Mama Herne closes the book. "What happened?"

I can still picture Ratchet falling down the Bottomless

Well. I claw at my throat, but the words don't come.

Mama Herne gets up. "Don't you worry on it," she says. "Some things are best left buried, that's what Papa Herne says."

There's a blackened pot resting on a flat stone close to the fire. She scoops a cup of its contents out for herself, then gestures for me to take the pot. "It's milk an' honey an' camomile flowers. It'll give you a good night's sleep, just you see."

As I drink it, all of the tiredness of the day – and the fear and excitement of the night – catch up with me. I glance up at the nest-homes in the trees. "Why are some of the Hob homes on branches and the others are on the ground by the fire?"

"A few of us like to live high up," says Mama Herne. "You get a different view of the world."

Minutes later, Papa Herne, Nissa and Half Crown return with a bundled blanket resting in Half Crown's antlers. As the tree-stag draws closer, I notice the felt blanket has small pieces missing. The cut-out shapes are of trousers and jackets and boots.

"Sorry about the missing pieces," says Papa Herne. "We'll patch it up for you. But for now, you can make do with these. They'll keep you warm."

Half Crown lowers the blanket bundle and unrolls it with his wooden snout. Inside is a heap of dry papery leaves and a wool sweater. The sweater is oversized, something I could grow into next year. There's a smell of earth as I pull it on. I gather the leaves and blanket around me, then lie down by the fire, listening to the soothing hiss of burning wood.

"I'm sorry about yer friend, an' all the others we left," says Papa Herne. "But it were too dangerous. Make no mistake, we might not have got away. Not in one piece anyways."

I can't find the words, but it feels as if part of me is still at Harklights, left behind with Petal.

"You'll like it here," adds Papa Herne. "Tomorrow, you'll get to meet the rest of the tribe an' I'll show you the forest."

I nod vaguely, wondering how the other Hobs will react. My eyelids grow heavy, then the fire and the forest slip away as sleep washes over me. For the first time ever, I'm not scared. I feel safe here, sheltered and protected, surrounded by a fortress of trees. It's how I imagine a home might feel.

CHAPTER FIVE

THE WANDWOOD TREE

I wake with a cry and sit bolt upright. Something small and warm and furry is trying to nestle into my armpit.

"Don't mind the dormice." Papa Herne smiles as the mouse scampers away. "They're friendly. We use them as bed warmers." He perches on a branch nearby. His felt clothes – blue-silver in moonlight, gold in firelight – look different now in the morning sun. It's as if they've been coloured by the forest. Bark-brown tunic and trousers, stone-grey hat, forest-green cloak. "Did you sleep well? You missed a beautiful dawn chorus."

"Yes, thanks." I don't know how long I've slept, but it's the best sleep I ever remember. The other orphans must be up already. I hope Petal is alright, hope Bottletop managed to get the hang of being a packsmith.

"Are you hungry? Mama Herne has made breakfast."

I catch a whiff of it then. Cooked eggs and mushrooms, like the stuff Old Ma Bogey cooks and keeps for herself and Padlock.

I scramble to my feet and brush off the leaves that have stuck to the smoke-grey sweater. The leaf bed was so much more comfortable than the floorboards. For once, cold hasn't crept into my bones.

The clearing is much bigger in the daylight, the sky-reaching trees much taller. A group of Hobs sit round the small fire, quietly eating from tiny plates and drinking from acorn bowls. There are more of them than I saw last night, thirty or so. All of them have the same nut-brown eyes and dark hair as Papa Herne. They look like one big family.

I kneel down so I'm not so giant-sized. I pull the sleeves of the sweater down to cover my knuckles.

"This is Wick, everyone," says Papa Herne. "The human boy I were telling you about."

"Pleased to meet you," answer the Hobs in a broken chorus.

Papa Herne smiles. "Here, let me introduce you to everyone. This is Nissa, who you met last night... An' that's Genna an' Finn an' their children Linden, Tiggs an' baby Tiya."

Finn holds a hand to his chest and adds, "Truly, we can never thank you enough for looking after her."

My heart feels full.

I nod as Papa Herne introduces all the Hobs, but I don't think I'll ever remember all their names.

"An' this is Nox." Papa Herne gestures to a bearded Hob sitting back from the fire circle. He wears the same green cloak as Papa Herne and Genna, but his acorn-coloured eyes don't have any of their glittering warmth.

He scowls and says, "What are you doing bringing a grown human to Oakhome? They're nothing but trouble an' bring destruction. What if other humans come looking for him?" He glances around at all the Hobs, looking for others who agree with him.

Papa Herne looks crossly at Nox. "Wick were abandoned. No one's coming for him. An' he's just a boy, he's not grown up."

"But he will be," Nox fires back in a crotchety voice. "We don't want humans here."

A murmur runs through the Hob tribe. I glance at their tiny nest-homes. They look fragile, like they would easily break if I accidentally stood or sat on them. I was right before, I am too big. I don't belong. I feel the eyes of the Hobs watching me, and swallow the knot in my throat. "Maybe I should go."

"Yeah, go," says Nox. "Yer bound to tread on young shoots an' seedlings."

"Yer not going anywhere," Papa Herne says to me, then he turns to Nox. "He kept Tiya safe from harm—"

"That's right," adds Nissa.

"—so we should hear what the wood sprites have to say about this." Papa Herne rubs his chin. "They can see his future. We'll take him after breakfast."

This is met with a chorus of agreement from some of the other Hobs.

Nissa looks stunned by the idea.

I wonder what the wood sprites are. Are they like Hobs?

Mama Herne is holding a tiny fire-blackened pan, sizzling with pieces of fried mushroom. Finn stirs the contents of a broken-topped hen's egg, which goes up to his waist, with a spoon that looks as if it's been carved from a bit of pine cone. He ladles out some of the cooked egg into an acorn bowl and adds a few grains of salt.

75

My mouth waters at the delicious cooking smells. And it's then that I realize I've not tasted anything but Old Ma Bogey's porridge in my whole life. It's true, I've imagined other foods, but never actually eaten anything else.

Mama Herne flips out the mushrooms onto a flat piece of scrubbed slate. "We don't have a plate your size. It's the best we could come up with."

"It's perfect," I say. I scoop up the mushrooms and pieces of egg and shovel them into my mouth. I close my eyes as the flavours burst over my tongue. I chew slowly, then swallow. The food is as good as it smells. No, it's even better.

"Would you like some more?"

I nod eagerly.

"Finn, Nissa," says Mama Herne. "Go to the cold store an' get me some more dried mushrooms an' loaves of bread."

"How many?" says Finn.

"All of them. Bring them in the wheelbarrow."

Both Finn and Nissa look shocked for a moment, but then they smile.

Minutes later, they return. The wheelbarrow, made from carved wood and an old cotton reel, is stacked with loaves of bread, each the size of the acorn-cradle.

"Go on, have as many as you like," says Mama Herne.

I take seven and eat them slowly, savouring the taste. The bread is so delicious I could wolf down the entire wheelbarrow-full, but I don't want to eat all of the Hobs' food.

I finish the tiny loaves, using the last one to mop the mushroom juices up.

Nissa's jaw drops at the sight of the empty slate. "You *are* hungry. Didn't they feed yer at the other place?"

"Not like this," I say through a mouthful of food, careful not to spray bits of it everywhere. I swallow and relish the mushroom-egg-bread taste. Porridge made with water and medicine might have given me all the minerals and stuff I needed, but it's not a patch on real food.

"Nox don't want to be carried," says Papa Herne as I pick him up on the palm of my hand. "He'll make his own way to see the wood sprites."

He nods towards what looks like a small hangar, nestled in the roots of a tree – something I'd not noticed last night. A blackbird, wearing a polished wooden saddle, sits under the shade of the hangar's curved bark roof. Nox climbs into the saddle before taking up the reins. Then the blackbird gets up, spreads its wings and takes off.

"Follow the winding earth track," says Papa Herne. "It's a path."

"Like the one we came in on last night?"

"Uh-huh. We call it Fox Path."

We leave the clearing and follow the path. Along the edge, green spears break through the dead leaves. We pass between towering trees, which must seem even more enormous to Papa Herne. There are no leaves yet, but I imagine them moving gently in a breeze, sunlight winking through the canopy overhead. I wonder if there are any cherry blossom trees. I've never seen one, but Petal likes to include them in her stories. She says the flowers are like clouds and the berries are sweet.

Apart from the bird calls, the forest is silent. Peaceful. There's no clock ticking off the minutes. No roar and rattle of the Machine.

Papa Herne's talk fills the silence as I walk. He goes from telling me how bees make honey, to primroses being the first flowers of spring, to the time his father went on an adventure downstream in a small wooden boat. I carry him upright in my fist, like I'd hold a candle, until my hand goes all clammy. Then I put him in my pocket next to my fast-beating heart.

After twenty minutes or so, we approach an ancient-looking ash tree. It stands far taller and wider than the other trees that grow close by, or the ones at Oakhome.

"We're here – this is the Wandwood Tree," says Papa Herne. "Home to the wood sprites."

The tree is hollow, bark has peeled away from one side and there's a foot-long gash at the base of the trunk. Nox's blackbird perches on a moss-covered root.

There are strange drawings on the peeled wood. Carved lines with patterns and mazes.

"Woodworms make them," says Papa Herne.

I put Papa Herne down and he walks straight through the opening, which to him must be like a big cave. He disappears inside. I crouch down, get on my knees and peer in.

The tree is hollowed out, but it's not empty. There's a low wooden table resting on a woven mat that covers the floor. Next to it is a papery thing with cubbyholes. Some of the cubbyholes are filled with dried flowers and scrolls and what look like small stones. On one of the walls is a shelf. Behind it, rising up, are more woodworm drawings. One is of a tree-man crowned with ivy and ferns and branches. Surrounding him is a whole forest of trees, birds and animals. All of this is lit by a shaft of sunlight, which reaches down from an opening, high up in the hollow trunk.

Nox sits cross-legged on the floor. He looks at us and says gruffly, "See you made it."

The place smells of wood and dry leaves.

"Come in, Wick," says Papa Herne.

At the edge of my eye, something flickers. I sense a presence just out of sight.

I hunker down on all fours and squeeze into the hollow. The top of the opening scrapes against my back, but I manage it. I straighten up and sit cross-legged on the matted floor, careful not to squash either of the Hobs. I glance up at the high ceiling, where wooden stalactites and a family of sleeping bats hang down, their wings like folded umbrellas.

On the shelf is a green glass lens shaped like a hexagon.

"This is where we come to sit an' get advice. The wood sprites are our guides."

I look up at the bats again. "Are they the wood sprites?" I whisper.

Papa Herne picks up the glass lens. It's as big as a serving tray in his hands. "Here, try looking through this."

I put the lens to my eye and jump up in shock, banging my head hard against one of the wooden stalactites.

We're not alone. Three winged figures – not much smaller than Papa Herne – glide through the air in front of me.

"Wood sprites," Papa Herne says.

My eyes water at the dull pain in the back of my head. The wood sprites have slender blue-green bodies, wild dark-green hair, dragonfly wings – and they are half transparent. I watch them in awe. I wish Petal could see this.

The wood sprites start to talk in high silvery voices that follow on from each other in bursts. "Papa Herne – great to see you – and who is this—"

They sound as if they are three people in one.

"I'm Wick." I suck air through my teeth as I feel the bump that's forming on the back of my head.

Nox makes a noise, clearing his throat. "Papa Herne found the boy outside the forest last night an' brought him home to live with us."

"A human boy – living – with the Hobs—" The sprites smile broadly at each other, exchanging meaningful looks. Only I don't know what the looks mean. And it doesn't seem as if Papa Herne or Nox do either.

"We came to ask about Wick," says Papa Herne. "Nox says humans are destructive an' we wanted to see what you thought about him living with us."

"Not all humans are destructive – humans have two sides – they can help or hurt—"

I squeeze my eyes shut and think of all the miniature matchstick models I built. Then I think about Old Ma Bogey burning them to ashes.

"The boy's future is not decided – it is up to him to choose his own path – as it is for all of you—"

I open my eyes. The sprites hover close to my face, watching me intently.

"Choices – make us into – who we are—"

This is their answer?

Papa Herne rubs his chin thoughtfully. "Well, I say we give him a chance."

I feel a shining bubble of excitement rise inside me. I want to burst out laughing, but I keep it in.

Nox covers his mouth and makes a grumbling sound. Then he gets up from the mat and leaves.

His disappointment doesn't change the way I feel.

"I know I'm big," I say to Papa Herne, "but I want to live with the Hobs and be part of the forest. I want to help and learn where magic comes from."

The sprites wheel through the air, their silvery voices

almost chanting now. "Wild magic – is the force – that makes everything grow—"

A picture of the barren earth at Harklights blooms in my mind. No wonder there was no magic and nothing grew there – it's an awful place.

I close my mind to the memory, let it fade. "Don't you, um, have any spell books? Things to learn from?"

The sprites change their flight. They swoop low, then carousel around us.

"Nature does not need books – only a staff or a wand – to focus the power—"

I wonder if magic could shrink me to the size of the Hobs. "Can magic make things smaller?"

Papa Herne frowns. "No, but you don't need to be small. As I said before, the forest is home to all sizes."

"It is true – all sizes – goodbye, Wick—"

The wood sprites rise up in the air above us and glide through the tree trunk as Papa Herne thanks them. We sit there for a few moments, then I glance to the tree-cave opening. "What about Nox?"

"Don't worry about him. He don't trust humans. He's always been like that, but he might change, given time."

I wonder what will happen if he doesn't.

CHAPTER SIX

FROGSPAWN

As I crawl out from the Wandwood Tree, the forest seems different. The birdsong isn't louder or quieter and the light is more or less the same. But I know there are wood sprites now – unseen, invisible things.

Nox stands by his blackbird, arms folded. "So he's staying?"

"Course Wick's staying," answers Papa Herne, his voice rising. "Long as he's not destructive—"

"An' if he is, then he goes?"

Papa Herne nods solemnly. "He goes."

Nox grumbles again as he climbs into his saddle.

"I'm gonna take Wick on a tour of the forest," adds Papa Herne. "Can you check on what we discussed earlier?"

"I've not forgot." Nox picks up his reins and flicks them.

His blackbird lifts its wings, then takes off, flying north.

Papa Herne watches till Nox and his bird are out of sight. "I think he's annoyed that the wood sprites didn't give him the answer he wanted. He wanted them to say you were like every other human, or the destructive ones." He pauses, and looks up at me. "But you aren't – or at least you don't have to be. Come on, let's go. We'll go back the way we came, then take Badger Path."

After a while, Papa Herne says, "We can stop here. Look."

He points to a thick tree with a hole at its base and a slope of scratched-out soil. A moment later, a fox cub appears, snuffling the air. His eyes are button-bright.

As Papa Herne climbs off my hand, other cubs appear. I've never seen animals like them. Their heads have black-and-white stripes, like humbugs. "What are they?"

"Badger cubs."

The three cubs clamber out of the hole and come close. Papa Herne walks up to them. They are huge next to him, like elephants standing by a man. He takes a flat leaf out of his jacket, holds it to his mouth and blows. A shrill whistle sound comes from the leaf. It startles me, but the cubs seem used to it.

A few moments later, a hare scampers out of the bushes and slows as it approaches us. Papa Herne tilts his hat. The hare nods in return, then lies down next to the cubs. Instantly they nuzzle the hare and begin feeding.

"Lost their mothers," Papa Herne says, watching them feed. "An' so us Forest Keepers look after them, make sure other animals feed them."

"Forest Keepers?"

Papa Herne tugs at his green cloak, which is clasped with a silver leaf. "Yeah. We're known by our cloaks. We take care of the forest. Patrol it an' protect it. Nature takes care of us by giving us food an' water an' a home. It's only right we take care of it in return. We might not be very tall, but small actions can make big differences."

"Why do you wear cloaks?"

"Cloaks are the cornerstone of Forest Keeping – a symbol of protection."

"How many Keepers are there?"

"There's me, Nox an' Genna. The other Hobs are Home Keepers – they stay an' look after Oakhome. They gather extra stores for the winter, in case any of the animals are low on food. Mostly it's nuts an' dried fruits."

The cubs have stopped feeding. I hold my hand out and the fox sniffs it cautiously.

"These are our Hob traditions. It's important to keep them, honour them, hold them tight."

The cubs bump their heads against my hand.

"Ah, I see you've got a way with animals," says Papa Herne. "There's a streak of wild in you."

Their soft coats slide under my fingers. I wonder if the cubs like me because they somehow sense that I know what it's like to be abandoned.

"You got the makings of a Forest Keeper, Wick." Papa Herne strokes the badger cubs and fox cub. "They love their bellies to be scratched," he says as they roll on their backs.

As we rub the fur on their bellies, Papa Herne smiles.

My heart feels as light as paper.

"Now the first thing you need to know about Forest Keeping is Forest Law. It's two unbreakable rules." He holds up his tiny hand and counts them off. "Number one, protect the forest. That means keeping things safe from harm, looking after sick birds an' animals, moving tree saplings to give them a better chance. Number two, never harm a living thing. That means things like not snapping live branches, or killing things. That's it. They're not many, but they cover everything."

A coldness creeps into me and I can't help thinking of how Old Ma Bogey got rid of orphans who didn't follow her rules. I shake my head and try to think about something else, to focus on the magic of my new home. "Are tree-stags how you usually get around the forest?"

"No."

"It must take you ages to walk everywhere."

"It does, but then we found a human boy to carry us." Papa Herne's face breaks into a smile. "I'm joking. Usually we ride on the backs of birds, foxes or badgers, but it's much easier to talk to you if you carry us."

I smile. Then I think of how big some of the animals are, how dangerous they could be to the Hobs. "Are you friends with all the animals in the forest?"

Papa Herne stops looking me in the eye. His smile fades and he becomes rigid. "Yeah, every single one." His voice sounds forced. I wonder if he's hiding something, but I can't think what.

He clears his throat. "Right, we best be off."

"Where are we going?" I pick him up and stroke the cubs one last time.

"We got other places to see."

We walk off down the path and head through a mess of rust-coloured bracken. I stop to pick up a small rock. It's squarish, flattened, like a jigsaw piece. Then I notice an indent in the path the exact same shape. I put the rock back where it belongs – it fits perfectly.

I'm struck by the quietness of the forest. There's no Machine thundering through the day. But there's a low hum. I look up, trying to see where it's coming from.

"What is it?" says Papa Herne.

"Buzzing."

"Honeybees," he replies. "You ever seen bees before?"

I shake my head. I've only seen pictures of them in the newspapers.

"Well, that needs to be changed." Papa Herne pulls on my thumb. "Come on, turn round, there's a change of plan. How's yer head for heights? There's a tree you need to climb."

I've been terrified of heights ever since I can remember. At the orphanage, there were nights when I'd wake up drenched in sweat. I'd have nightmares of falling down the Bottomless Well. Just like Flint and Ratchet and many others. Falling for ever and ever.

But I don't want to disappoint Papa Herne, not on my first day in the forest. It's clear he has no problem with heights as he's being carried in the palm of my hand. It must be like standing on a roof or the prow of a ship to him.

When we reach the tree I'm supposed to climb, the air above us is filled with a loud humming. I look up and see something hanging from one of the high branches, like an overgrown nut. It's so high up, fear tingles through my toes.

As I put my free hand on the bark, my palms break out in a sweat.

"I don't think I can climb. I'm no good with heights."

"It don't matter," says Papa Herne. "We can try another time."

There isn't any disappointment in his words, but I can't help feeling as useless as a wet match.

"Let's go back to Oakhome, I got some things to do. You can go off with Nissa, Linden an' Tiggs, an' play."

Play. The idea feels strange. I know it's something children enjoy, but at Harklights playing and games were forbidden. We were only allowed to sit about in the yard or the dormitory, looking at pictures, listening to Petal or drawing with chalk.

On the way back, we come across a group of hens digging around in the old leaves.

"They're looking for seeds an' insects," says Papa Herne.

Above the hens, high in the bare branches, are what look like more nest-homes. There are dozens of them. My toes ache just at the thought of how far up they are. I ask Papa Herne if there's another tribe of Hobs who live there.

Papa Herne blinks hard a few times. He tugs at the

collar of his cloak to get more air. "Hmm. No, it's mistletoe. It's a plant that grows with a tree, like we grow with the forest."

I'm starting to get the feeling that Papa Herne is holding something back.

He tugs at his collar again and won't meet my eyes.

He's acting a little strangely. I want to ask him if everything is alright, but I don't want to upset anything. So I swallow the question as it climbs in my throat.

When we get back to Oakhome, several Hobs are using a thimble to water small pieces of fabric with moss growing on them. Another group are carving wooden tools using a horn-handled razor and a nail file.

Mama Herne and Finn are preparing tonight's meal. Nissa is helping, but after Papa Herne whispers something in her ear, she brightens, puts down her miniature kitchen utensils and comes over.

"What games d'you know?" she says. "We got lots of winged seeds. Can you play whirligigs?"

I scratch my neck. "We weren't allowed to play games at Harklights."

"Oh," says Nissa. Her face falls in disappointment.

"I, er, did like seeing the animals today."

Nissa's eyes light up. "Then we could go an' see the frogspawn. It's come early. That means it's spring."

"Frog what?"

"Frog*spawn*. It's their eggs." Nissa glances across to Linden and Tiggs. "Only, we'll have to take those two with us."

I glance over to the young Hobs, who are chasing each other around some slow-moving snails. Linden only comes up to Nissa's shoulders and Tiggs is even smaller. The snails, nearly as tall as Tiggs, are leaving thick tracks of slime. The young Hobs are careful not to tread in it.

"Let's do it," I say.

"Come on, you two," Nissa calls to Linden and Tiggs. "We're going to the deer pond!"

Both of them stop. Tiggs lets out a moan. "But I want to stay an' play with my snails!"

"You can play with them again later," says Nissa evenly.

Linden jumps over a trail of slime and runs over to Nissa. Tiggs picks up something from the ground and follows. He stands alongside the others and stares up at me. "Tuff is coming too."

"Tuff is his toy squirrel," says Linden before I can ask. "He goes everywhere with him."

"*I* wanted to tell him about Tuff!" Tiggs knocks into Linden and holds up a tiny carved squirrel. "Carry us in yer hand, like you carried Papa Herne."

"If it's no trouble," adds Linden.

I put my outstretched hand to the ground and pick them up carefully.

"You've got buttons!" adds Tiggs. "Genna finds them for me. I collect them – they're treasure."

"Where does she find them?"

Tiggs shrugs. "I dunno."

"Where d'you think yer going?" says Mama Herne.

"The deer pond," replies Nissa, peering down from my hand.

Mama Herne frowns and folds her arms. "You know yer supposed to stay round here."

Nissa's shoulders drop. "But it's not far, Mama. Wick wanted to see the frogspawn. He's never seen it before."

Mama Herne considers this for a moment. Then her frown disappears. "Alright, but you be careful an' be back before sundown."

"We will," chorus the Hob children.

"Nissa, don't you go using that catapult," adds Papa Herne. "An' keep an eye on the boys, both of you."

Nissa nods.

"Don't worry," I say. "I'll take care of them."

We leave the clearing and head south along a thin worn path. Along the way, Nissa and Linden make bird whistles with their hands and call down a family of sparrows from the trees. I try to whistle but I can't get it right. Neither can Tiggs.

The deer pond isn't far. The murky surface is a darkish mirror, reflecting bare branches and sky and clouds. By the edge is a scatter of lily pads and a lumpish clump of jelly.

"Frogspawn!" says Nissa.

I carefully put the Hob children down and they race over to the water's edge.

"There are hundeds," says Tiggs.

"Yes, hundereds," says Linden.

"Won't be long before they hatch into tadpoles," says Nissa. "Then they become little frogs with tails. I love watching them. When they're young, they're always changing."

"I can't wait for them to turn into froggers," says Tiggs, clapping his hands. "Then we can play hopper!"

I lie on my front to get as close to the frogspawn as the Hobs and take in all the details. It's beautiful – the bubbles of jelly are like clear berries with black seeds in the middle. I run my hand over them, then lift my dripping fingers out of the water. The droplets make circles in the water, circles that grow bigger and bigger.

After several minutes, two insects come darting out from the reeds and drift closer.

"Pond skaters," says Nissa.

"They walk on water," I say, surprised.

"Skate," corrects Nissa. "They're amazing."

I smile. "Everything is amazing here."

We watch the pond skaters dart across the mirrored surface. Their outstretched feet make little dents on the water. Linden and Tiggs jump around, pretending to be frogs.

"Tiggs! Come away from there!" says Nissa, when he gets close to the lily pads. "I don't want you falling in the pond. You can't swim, remember?"

"Yeah," echoes Linden. "Be careful!"

I smile and sigh. I'm pleased the Hobs let me stay. More and more, the forest feels like it could be a home. I think I might be happy here.

CHAPTER SEVEN

THE FOREST KEEPER

Linden and Tiggs return to playing frogs away from the water's edge. I catch my reflection in the still surface. An orphan boy looks back at me: underfed, angled cheekbones. I might have escaped Harklights, but it feels as it's left its mark, engraving me on the inside. I wince at my reflection, then look away, up at the trees that surround the pond. Their moss-covered roots, trunks and branches are soothing to my eyes. Something amber-coloured glows with sunlight on one of the trees. It looks like a forest jewel.

"Is it honey?" I say to Nissa as I walk over, carrying her in my hand.

"Tree sap. Papa calls it Nature's Glue."

"Hmm. That gives me an idea." I press a finger against the nugget of tree sap until it bursts. Oozes.

Then I set Nissa down and grab several twigs and glue them together the same way I glued matches.

Nissa glances up at me. "What are you making? Is it a hut? It's really good."

"Thanks." It feels awkward and strange. As if I'm showing Nissa a wound that hasn't healed. "I used to, er, make model buildings. They were my dreams of homes made real."

"What d'you mean?"

My throat is dry as paper. "They were places I hoped that one day I'd get to live in." As Nissa watches me add another twig I feel my cheeks flush. "I never let any of the others see them, except Petal."

I can't believe I'm saying all this. The walls I put up to protect myself are falling down.

"It's okay to keep things for yerself, you know," Nissa says. "I mean, I don't go around telling everyone I want to be a Forest Keeper—"

"You do?"

Nissa's eyes go wide. She's said more than she wanted.

Now it's her turn to blush. "I, er, yeah…since always." She sighs and glances over at Linden, who's running after Tiggs. "Linden wants to be a Home Keeper, like his father. Bake bread. Grow food. Gather firewood with the help of foxes. I want to be like my father too, but I'm not allowed."

"You want to be Hob leader?"

Nissa's flush deepens. "I didn't mean, I – he wants me to help look after Linden an' Tiggs. But I want to protect the forest an' look after the animals. He only let me come along to rescue Tiya as a one-off…"

Nissa pulls a tiny rock from a pouch tied to her belt. She takes a deep breath, holds the catapult up, draws back on the elastic and aims. Then she fires.

Crack.

The rock hits a pine cone on the forest floor, sending it skittering away.

I glue another twig into place. The twig-hut grows as I tell Nissa about my life at Harklights: Flint's wicked smile after he stole Old Ma Bogey's thumb-guard, Petal's dark eyes twinkling as she told stories, Wingnut's chalk drawings of the places he remembered. I get a warm feeling thinking about them. Even though I don't know if any of the orphans snitched on me to Old Ma Bogey,

I still miss them. Broken pieces of family put together. The closest thing to a family I have ever known. Maybe they're thinking of me too. Maybe they're wondering if I'm okay, beyond the wall. I hope no one else has gone down the Well.

"It's a shame that Petal didn't escape too, she looked nice."

A surge of guilt runs through me. "You would like her, she's great."

"Sometimes I miss not having other Hobs my own age around." Nissa takes another rock from her pouch.

"Have you always lived in the forest?"

"Yeah, I grew up here. There used to be more of us. There were other Hob villages in Sixways Wood, not far from here. But then, when I were seven, everyone who lived there disappeared."

"Really?" Nissa's words worry me.

She fires off another shot.

Crack.

"Disappeared? What do you mean?"

"They just left their homes an' went. No one knows why. An' then a few nights before you arrived, I overheard Papa an' Nox talking about a monster prowling."

104

"A *monster*?"

"Somewhere near Havenwood Forest. They were afraid it were getting closer an' closer. They stopped talking when they realized I were listening—"

"*Help!*" The cry comes from Linden. He stands rigid at the edge of the pond. The surface by the lily pads ripples, making the reflected trees sway.

"Where's Tiggs?" shouts Nissa.

"He fell in..." Linden's eyes are wide with shock.

I don't think to take off my boots but climb straight into the pond. The water is about a foot deep. I wade cautiously over to where Tiggs last was, afraid I might step on him.

"He can't swim! Do something!" yells Nissa. Her shrill voice scares the birds. They take to the sky, making alarm calls.

I cast about, frantically searching the water.

I feel a flash of hope as I see Tuff bobbing on his side on the surface, then it's gone – Tiggs is nowhere to be seen.

Fear crashes through me. I gasp for breath. This isn't happening.

Then I spot Tiggs lying in the murky water at the bottom of the pond.

He's not moving.

My chest tightens as I plunge my hands in and scoop him up. I don't know what to do, so I lay him carefully on the ground. His felt clothes and boots are soaked, heavy, swollen with water. A puddle pools around him as Nissa drops to his side. She shakes him and thumps him on the back. "Tiggs, wake up!"

Tiggs coughs up a mouthful of water, then coughs

again. Nissa helps him to sit upright and pushes the hair back from his face.

A slick of snot runs from his nose to his mouth. He wipes it away with his tongue and looks up at me. "Can I have one of yer buttons?"

Nissa makes a sound somewhere between a sob and a laugh. "He's alright."

As I let out a deep breath, Linden rushes over and hugs his brother until he's soaked too. It looks as if they both fell in.

I pluck the lowest button off my shirt, near the bit I tore to make the acorn-baby nappy, and give it to Tiggs. Then I fetch Tuff from the pond.

"We can't tell Papa Herne," says Nissa firmly. "We must keep it a secret."

Linden chews his lip. "I have to tell him the truth. He says we got to."

Nissa's eyes fill with more worry. "Please, Linden. Tiggs'll get into trouble."

Tiggs says nothing and hugs his toy squirrel.

Linden shakes his head. "No, it'll be you an' Wick that will get in trouble. You were meant to keep an eye on us."

My chest tightens again. I feel bad for not keeping my word about looking out for Tiggs. This was my one chance at finding a home. Now it's slipping away through my fingers. That's it, I think. I'll be back at Harklights by dinner time.

After Nissa wrings the water out of Tiggs's jacket and trousers and wraps him and Linden in dry leaves, we decide to go back to Oakhome. I carry the Hob children in my hands again. They are as light as matches, but there's a heavy feeling in my stomach. Mostly we don't say anything.

I play out different paths for how the conversation might go when we get back. All of them lead to me being sent back to the orphanage.

I tell myself I'm not really bothered if they want me gone. I didn't ask for them to take me in. And how good would life in the forest be anyway? I try to ignore how beautiful the speckled sunlight makes everything look.

Sparrows call out from the upper branches, but we don't make bird whistles again. Instead, we listen to their song and the silence of the trees.

As we arrive at Oakhome, Mama Herne, Finn and the other Home Keepers are cooking dinner in a set of tiny metal pots. Nox sits away from them, hunched forward and brooding.

Mama Herne takes one look at us and says, "How come the boys are all wet?"

My stomach twists.

Nissa's shoulders drop. "Tiggs fell in the water," she says before Linden can say anything.

"I'm alright," says Tiggs. "Look – Wick gave me one of his buttons!"

"Quick, get them by the fire an' get them dry clothes," says Mama Herne. "They'll catch their death of cold."

Finn drops his wooden spoon and gets moss-grown blankets to wrap round them. Genna and several other Hobs race off to one of the huts.

Nissa bites her lip. "He nearly drowned but Wick went in an' saved him."

"What?" Papa Herne's eyes flash with anger. "You were s'posed to look out for him!"

"We were," I say, clearing my throat, looking to the ground and wishing I didn't stand out so much. "We turned away for a minute."

I wait for Papa Herne to start shouting.

"He went on the lily pads." Linden hugs the blanket around him. "He were trying to touch the frogspawn."

"What did I tell you?" says Nox, getting up from his seat, his voice rising. "Told you the boy would bring trouble."

I brace myself for what comes next – Papa Herne saying it was a bad idea that I live with them, telling me to go.

"First rule of Forest Keeping is to protect the forest." Nox jabs his finger at me. "That includes Hobs."

Papa Herne looks at me sharply. "Yer very lucky Tiggs didn't drown. Wick, if you are gonna stay with us, you got to stick to Forest Law."

"I – I – will," I stutter, stumbling over my words.

"I'll make an exception this once, but if you break one of the rules..." Papa Herne turns to Nissa. "An' you, you were supposed to be keeping an eye on Tiggs too."

Nissa bows her head. "Sorry, Papa."

"He broke a rule, he should go," says Nox gruffly.

"Hold on, Nox," says Papa Herne. "I've not even started training him yet."

I open my mouth to say something, but I can't think what to say.

"He has to go. He'll bring destruction!"

"We don't know that."

"Are you gonna train Wick to be a Forest Keeper?" says Nissa.

She sounds as surprised as I am. Papa Herne said I would make a good Forest Keeper, but he never said anything about training.

Forest Keeper.

There's a stab of guilt. This is what Nissa wants.

"I could do with someone to cover the South-East Quarter." Papa Herne nods at me encouragingly. "Wick shows great potential."

"Let's face it," says Nox, "he's already failed once. It's just a matter of time before he fails again."

Nissa's mouth draws into a thin line. She walks away towards Mama Herne, who's wiping her hands down her apron and giving her a stern look.

"Thanks for, er, showing me the frogspawn," I say, calling after Nissa.

She doesn't turn around.

All of the Hobs are gathered in a half circle round the fire, sitting on twigs as if they are benches. I sit down on the ground opposite, but still feel too big, so I hunch forward, trying to make myself smaller. My wet boots and socks are close to the fire. Steam rises from them. We eat a dinner of something called nut roast and dried apricots with cheese. Each nut roast is like a matchbox-sized loaf of bread. I eat twelve of them.

"Where does all the food come from?" I say.

"The forest," replies Papa Herne. "We got our own hens for eggs, hares for milk, we grow some vegetables an' collect mushrooms, nuts an' fruits. An' some of the things are human things we found. That's where we got the blanket from an' yer sweater."

"An' the salt an' sugar," adds Mama Herne.

"Do you have contact with humans?" I ask.

There's silence. Nox bristles at the word "humans". Then Papa Herne says, "There's not been any in the forest. Not since we moved here anyways. An' we prefer to be by ourselves. Everything – mostly everything – we need is here." After a moment, he turns to the other Hobs and says, "Who wants a story?"

"I do!" cries Tiggs.

"How about how the magpie stole away Tiya?" offers Mama Herne. "An' how Wick looked after her."

The Hobs cheer.

I feel a hint of warmth in my chest. They want me to stay. At least, most of them do.

Nox picks up his tiny plate, gets up and leaves the clearing.

Papa Herne stands on a branch and raises his voice. "Once there were a Hob couple called Genna an' Finn Knowle. They had three children: Linden, Tiggs an' Tiya. Tiya were the youngest, only a few months old…"

All eyes are fixed on Papa Herne as he spins his story. "…Genna took the acorn-cradle an' polished it. One morning, when Tiya were asleep in the cradle, the sun shined on the wood so bright it looked like a diamond. A greedy magpie in a nearby tree saw the shining an' thought it were a jewel…"

Tiggs hugs Tuff tight, when Papa Herne tells how the magpie snatched Tiya's cradle and Nissa alerted everyone. He holds Tuff even tighter as Papa Herne tells how they flew on their blackbirds, chasing the magpie to Harklights. When the story reaches the part where I find Tiya and look after her, the Hobs peer up at me, smiling brightly. A small part of me wonders what would have happened if Petal had escaped too. If she had been with us, we would have had an extra pair of eyes and

Tiggs might not have nearly drowned.

After Papa Herne finishes the story, the Hobs leave the fire circle and head to their nest-huts. Squirrels carry the ones who live up on the branches.

"Petal told stories back at Harklights…" I say, as Papa Herne climbs down from his branch.

He looks up at me. "Stories are a way of remembering who we are, but also a way of finding out who we want to be."

I lie under the felt blanket on a bed of leaves, watching the flames curl round the firewood. I think again about Papa Herne training me instead of Nissa, and what he said about sticking to Forest Law. My first day in the forest didn't go as I expected. I only just found out about Forest Law and then I go and break one of the rules. I didn't protect Tiggs. I don't want to be a destructive human that hurts things. All I want is to help and make things better. All my life, I've been part of the Machine, separated from nature. This is my time to be something different. I want to be a Forest Keeper.

Several dormice scuttle across the clearing and snuggle up by my shoulder.

I think about what Nissa said about the disappearing

Hobs, about losing her friends. Maybe I could find them. Maybe this could be a way to show Papa Herne and everyone – even Nox – that I really can help.

Now, as I close my eyes, I try and come up with a plan. But I don't know where to begin – all I can think about are the disappearing Hobs and Petal. And a monster prowling.

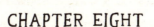

CHAPTER EIGHT

LEAF HUNTING

There are lots of different paths across the forest. Wide winding paths. Narrow paths edged with heather or bracken. Sunken paths with high rising sides that are more like tunnels. Faint paths that are nothing more than a thin trail of churned-up leaf mulch. Papa Herne shows me all of these from his perch on the palm of my hand as he guides me on another tour of the forest.

As we walk, I think back to the wood sprites. Are there more of them here, unseen, gliding about in the forest air, disappearing into tree trunks and flowers? I wish I'd borrowed the hexagonal lens, so I could see them.

"Are the sprites ghosts?"

"If you mean were they living an' died, then no. They've always been spirits."

We pass close to three deer. A stag, a doe and a younger doe. They stop and watch us. I wait for them to race away, but they are curious and brave. They draw closer; the young doe raises its head and whuffles at my sleeve.

"Stay calm. She's just getting yer scent, there we go."

I wonder if she can smell Harklights on me.

"Now you can stroke her. That's it – slowly."

The deer fur is warm, soft. It's coarser than that of the orphan cubs, but nothing like the bark of Half Crown.

"We give them extra food in winter. We got underground stores, not far from Oakhome."

The other doe trots over and bumps me gently with her head.

Stroking the deer calms me. All of my worries – about Papa Herne training me instead of Nissa, about Nox not wanting me to stay – fade like photographs left out in the sun. What was it Papa Herne said? I have a way with animals. Maybe this is a sign that I sort of belong here.

"Where in the forest do the deer live?" I ask.

"Most of them prefer to live northwards, on Wayland Heath," answers Papa Herne. "Beyond the edge of the forest, past Lightning Rock."

"Are we going to visit them?"

"No, no, no!" he says quickly, breaking out in a sweat. "The North is a wild place that's just for them. We keep away so we don't disturb them." He flexes a shoulder as if he's trying to shake something off.

The feeling that Papa Herne is hiding something comes rushing back. He's definitely uneasy. Maybe there's something bad in the North. I make a note of it in my mind. It could be important.

As we visit other parts of the forest – Beech Hanger with its steep downslope, and a gorge by an old mine – the idea of going back to rescue Petal starts to take shape. I'll go back alone; it'll be safer. I don't want anything happening to the Hobs. As I think about the orphanage wall, fear rises inside me. There's no way I'm going over the top. I'll have to sneak through the gates with one of the food deliveries. But what if I get caught? Or Petal gets caught trying to escape again? Both of us are bound to go down the Bottomless Well. The thought sends a shiver through me. But it doesn't change anything. I must go back. I know I can't leave her there.

The next day I wake to the sound of birdsong. Sunlight streams into the clearing. It still feels good not waking up to Old Ma Bogey thrashing the gong, as if it's an orphan who woke her in the night. There's a wonderful smell of something sweet baking. I get up to investigate.

A group of baker Hobs are taking a brick-sized loaf of bread out from a clay oven, which is framed by the roots of a broken oak stump. Nearby, a fox appears with a hen's egg in its mouth and drops it into a pot of boiling water. I can't remember seeing the oven yesterday and wonder if it just appeared by magic. Papa Herne, Mama Herne, Finn and some others are busy with even more preparations. Linden is with them, covered with a light dusting of flour. It reminds me of the time Flint covered himself in chalk and pretended to be the ghost of an orphan who went down the Bottomless Well. Old Ma Bogey was furious. She beat him till the air filled with clouds of chalk dust.

"Um, what are you making?" I ask.

"Honey cakes," says Papa Herne, looking up. "Quarter Day is coming up the day after tomorrow. There are four of them in the year. They're when we celebrate each season. This time it's Bring Forth."

I stretch. "Bring *Forth*?"

"Yeah, it's spring. Seeds sprout, tree buds unfold, birds make nests and animals ready dens for their young. New beginnings." He pauses, smiles. "Looks like you came along at the right time."

"Thought you might like a bigger loaf," says Finn. "I don't know what it'll be like though. I've not made bread so big before."

"It smells delicious," I say. My stomach aches, and I realize how hungry I am. "Do you want any help?"

"No, no. You go an' sit," adds Finn. "It needs a few minutes to cool down. Linden'll call you when it's ready."

Linden nods proudly.

When I sit with Nissa and Tiggs for breakfast, Nox is sat close by, talking with several other Hobs. The rest of the Hobs sit around the fire, eating slices of tiny Hob-sized bread with smidges of scrambled egg and mushroom.

Nox raises his voice so I can hear him. "How's he gonna look after the forest? He said he can't even climb a tree. What happens if there's a sick bird up in a high nest? He can't go an' fly up there on a blackbird."

The Hobs he's sitting with look up to see my reaction.

"What d'you think Papa Herne sees in him?" says one of them.

Nox scratches his beard. "I dunno."

His words sting. Colour rises in my cheeks. I want to tell him that I don't know either. He's right. So much of the forest is off the ground. If anything needs help up a tree, there's not much I can do.

"Leave him alone," says Nissa.

"What's it to you?" Nox scowls at Nissa. "Aren't you meant to be washing acorn cups or looking after Tiya or something?"

"Ignore him," says Nissa to me.

I'm surprised. I guess she isn't upset with me any more.

When the loaf is ready, I tear off a thick wedge and put it on my slate with the boiled egg and a heap of cooked mushrooms. The eggshell is still hot – I peel it quickly. The bread is delicious.

Tiggs watches me, open-mouthed. "Look at how much he eats!"

"Stop staring at him," says Nissa. "He's got feelings, you know. Go see if Linden wants some help."

"Okay," replies Tiggs, running off with his toy squirrel.

"I don't mind," I say, biting into the boiled egg. "Thanks for, you know, sticking up for me just now."

"Nox isn't worth worrying about. You'll get used to him. He's just…"

"You okay with me being trained?" I say without thinking.

Nissa's mouth makes a tight smile. "I'm fine. I just wish Papa had taken me to see the wood sprites. They could have seen my future, told me what I were meant to do too. I mean, what if I'm actually meant to be a Forest Keeper?"

"Why don't you ask him to take you?"

She glances at Papa Herne, who's over by the bird hangar. "I can't. He's our leader. I got to do what he wants. It's not bad. I just wish I got to choose – like you did."

"I can say something to Papa Herne—"

"There's no point," Nissa interrupts. "He wants to hold onto tradition. Words aren't gonna change his mind."

I walk for ages, following Papa Herne, who's riding his blackbird this time. It alights on branches, moss-covered rocks and the forest path ahead as it waits for me to catch up. The land rises and falls. We stop where a small tree-covered hill is peppered with holes. Several rabbits sit near them, completely still, their ink-black eyes watchful.

"This is where the rabbits live," he says. "Best watch where you walk though. You don't want to step on a rabbit hole covered in leaves. You might injure yer foot."

"I'll be careful," I say, noticing a half-hidden rabbit hole a few feet away.

"Rabbit homes are called warrens."

"Warrens," I repeat.

Papa Herne nods. "That's right. They like eating flowers an' grass an' clovers. Though they can't eat bracken or foxgloves – it makes them sick."

"Fox *gloves*?"

"It's a type of flower."

"And is bracken a flower too?"

"No, no, it's a plant." Papa Herne takes off his hat and runs a hand through his dark hair. "Maybe I should go more slowly. I forgot you don't know much about the forest."

"I know some things," I say.

Papa Herne's smile turns into a twinkle in his eyes. "We should start with the trees. Trees are always a good place to begin. Trees are like yer clocks. Their shadows tell the time of day, their leaves the seasons."

We examine the shapes of deciduous trees. We look at their outlines first, the shapes their bare branches make. Rounded oak, elm, beech. Oval ash and birch. We then move onto leaves. As the new leaves aren't out yet, we hunt for old ones in the leaf litter on the forest floor. Lobed oak leaves. Eye-shaped beech leaves. Tooth-edged birch and hornbeam leaves. They feel like paper between my fingers.

"Evergreens an' conifers are next," says Papa Herne, climbing into his saddle and picking up the reins.

"Aren't you afraid of heights? When you're up in the trees?"

"A bit of fear is a good thing – it can keep us alive." Papa Herne touches his hat. "But too much can stop us living."

As I get to my feet, his blackbird skirrs into the air with swift wingbeats, then glides to land on another branch. Bright sunlight makes a mosaic on the forest floor. I step from sunspot to sunspot, as if they are stepping stones and the shade is water.

When I hear a tapping sound, not far off in the trees, I stop by an oak.

Papa Herne flies back and lands in branching shadows by my feet. "Why are we stopping?"

"What's that knocking?"

We wait.

The tapping starts again.

"Woodpecker," says Papa Herne.

I crane my neck to look at the upper branches of the oak. My fingers trace the ridges of the trunk's grey bark. "How hard is it to climb a tree?" I think of the Bottomless Well and Old Ma Bogey. She's the reason I'm afraid of heights, afraid to fall. Why should I let her hold me back? I tighten my jaw.

"You don't have to do this. We got time enough."

"If I'm going to be fully part of the forest, I need to climb." I clench my insides and fold back the sleeves of my sweater. "I want to do this now."

"Alright. But we can use something to help." He points his staff to a patch of ivy on the ground.

I watch in wonder as a burst of green light shoots out and a tremor runs through the leaves.

A thick cord of ivy vine races across the forest floor, then climbs and winds around the oak until it reaches the crown. Then it tumbles down from a high branch.

I remember Half Crown twisting and transforming with wild magic. "Can you turn trees into other things instead of tree-stags?" I ask.

"Tree-stags are traditional."

"Could you turn the whole forest into tree-stags?"

"I wouldn't have the energy. Magic takes a good deal

of concentration. I'm still learning from the wood sprites. Mostly I use it to help seedlings an' other plants to settle when I move them—"

When the ivy reaches me, it winds round my waist, tendrils corkscrewing around themselves.

"—an' use it to lift heavy objects. There we go. Now, look for knots and whorls, bark-holes and nubs. Anything you can use for a hand- or foothold."

I reach up for a knot and get a firm grip, then find a foothold on a curve of bark.

"That's it." Papa Herne points his staff at the slack ivy cord, which tightens. "If you slip yer not gonna fall. You'll just hang in the air."

"Do you climb trees yourself?"

"Occasionally...takes ages though. Never when it rains. You can't climb wet trees. Now, see that branch there?" Papa Herne points to one nearby. "Reach up with yer hand an' test its strength."

I grab the branch and tug it. It doesn't move.

"You can tell the strength of a branch by its size. An' check for lichen. D'you know what that is?"

"No."

"They're circles of crust – they look a bit like scabs.

Branches that are completely covered in lichen are dead an' will snap easily. Unless there's leaf growth on them. Remind me to show you. Now, find yer footing an' shift yer weight."

I follow his instructions. Even with the ivy rope clinging to me, I'm still dreading it. Blood roars in my ears. My fingers tremble and palms sweat as I climb. This isn't like climbing stairs. You don't always know where to put your feet.

Papa Herne and his blackbird flit from branch to branch. "Yer doing fine," says Papa Herne. "Take yer time."

As I secure my right foot on a hold, it slips. My leg slides down against the trunk.

All at once, my weight is being held by my fingers.

I'm going to fall.

The thought is overwhelming. Fear floods through me. The strength goes out of my legs.

I glance down, wide-eyed, as I lose my grip—

And fall backwards—

Maybe ten feet—

Then the ivy cord snaps tight, dangling me upside down over the forest floor.

My heart knocks hard against my chest. My hands shake worse than Bottletop's.

"Yer alright!" hollers Papa Herne when his bird lands on a branch close to me.

"Get me down," I say, trying to keep the fear out of my voice.

Papa Herne magics the ivy to lower me to the ground. "You did good. You were very brave. But next time, we should try with a smaller tree."

CHAPTER NINE

NEST MAKERS

We head back to Oakhome and find ourselves by the deer pond. The water is clear again, a mirror reflecting the sky. I think back to what Nissa said before Tiggs fell in. "What happened to the Hobs who disappeared?" I say.

"You know about that?"

"Not really. Nissa mentioned it."

"It were five years ago now, in the summer. Nox an' I went to Ferngrove in Sixways Wood, where we used to live."

"Is that past Lightning Rock?"

"No, but it's not too far away." He takes a deep breath and tugs at his cloak. "Anyways, when we got to Ferngrove, everyone had disappeared. Then we went to Owls Hatch and Briarbank, the other Hob villages in the wood, an' it were the same. We tried looking for everyone, followed tracks. Thought they might have moved... but..." He taps his staff. "We found nothing. None of them came back."

A shiver runs through me. It's as if he's talking about the Bottomless Well.

"Nissa said she heard you say something about a monster."

Papa Herne flinches, uncomfortable at my words. "I don't know what she's talking about," he says quickly. "She must have heard wrong, I'm sure."

He's definitely hiding something, but then I am too, I realize. I clear my throat. "Old Ma Bogey had a dead Hob in a bell jar. I meant to tell you."

Papa Herne looks at me intently. "Is that right?"

I remember the framed box filled with butterflies. "Maybe she's behind them disappearing."

He frowns. "There's not been any disappearances in a long time. But we should keep an eye out for anything that don't look right."

My eye catches on a band of sparrows gathered on nearby branches, with twigs and leaves in their beaks. At first there are five or six, but soon there are twenty

or more. Then other birds join them: wood pigeons, song thrushes, chaffinches, jays.

"What are they doing?"

Papa Herne raises his hat to them. "Making a nest," he says.

As the sun blazes overhead, we make our way back, lost in our own thoughts. I'm unsettled knowing there might be a monster making the Hobs disappear. What if it's still out there – some vicious beast, like from one of Petal's stories? All of the trees that surround us and usually make me feel safe and protected now feel different. The spaces between them are filled with doubt. I find myself looking for paw prints and prowling shapes.

When we reach Oakhome, the Hobs are bowling with pill woodlice on the forest floor. Papa Herne asks me to join in, but I stay at the edge of the clearing. Nissa sits alongside me on a cushion of moss. We watch the woodlice roll, watch some of them unfold and scurry away. Linden and Tiggs chase after them.

"I asked him about the Monster," I say to Nissa, dragging a stick through the leaf litter to make a line.

Nissa's eyes brighten. "What did he say?"

"He said you must have heard him wrong, but I think he's hiding something."

"That's because he *is* hiding something." Nissa stands up. "We should see if we can find out what he's not telling us. You can see if there's anything unusual when you're out with Papa Herne an' I can check Nox's nest-hut for clues."

"Why Nox's hut?"

"His wife was one of the Hobs who disappeared."

Her words hit me. "I didn't know." I realize that Nox nearly always seems to be on his own, unlike the rest of the Hobs.

"She were away from Oakhome, on a picnic..." Nissa swallows. "If we find out anything, we'll tell each other.

Right?" She reaches out a hand.

"Right." I reach out my thumb. It's not exactly a handshake, but it's good enough for us.

Nissa steps over to the line I've drawn. "I think the answer is in the North, beyond where Nox and Genna patrol. Where only the deer are allowed."

"Papa Herne got really flustered when I asked him about going beyond Lightning Rock. There must be something there. Or Sixways Wood, where the abandoned villages are."

"Yeah." Nissa smiles. "Whatever it is, we're gonna find out. It's good to have you as a friend. Even if you are so big."

"I can't help it," I say, making myself lower.

"Yeah, well don't go growing up any more."

When Linden and Tiggs bring the runaway woodlice back, Finn wraps his sons in his arms and hugs them tight. It hurts to see how much the Hob parents love their children.

I wonder how long the dream of living at Oakhome will last – if one day I'll wake up at Harklights on the dormitory floor covered in chalk dust, surrounded by smudged drawings of trees and birds and little people.

Papa Herne doesn't say anything about yesterday's failed climb when we head out into the forest. He flies ahead on his blackbird again. This time, as well as flitting from rock to roots and bough to branch, his bird boldly lands on my outstretched arm. It weighs no more than a couple of matchboxes. I wonder what the other orphans are doing right now. They're probably packing matchboxes. This is my fourth day away from Harklights. I feel a pull to go back for Petal, but I'm not ready. Not just yet. I need to be strong enough. To make sure Old Ma Bogey doesn't win this time.

After visiting the Milk Hare and the cubs, we follow Badger Path south, heading towards the southern end of Deer Path. I carry Papa Herne and his bird perched on my wrist. He tells me about patrol skills and how to read the forest.

"It's not all the same," he says. "Not when you look closely."

He points out the details of things I would have just called "forest". Birch stalks cloaked to their throats in woolly apple-green moss. Scraggly ivy. Ranks of young nettles. Trees scuffed where deer have rubbed their antlers against them. A sunken amphitheatre, where the ground has collapsed on itself and revealed a ten-foot ledge dotted with large holes – a cross-section of burrows. Only they're not just details, they're markers too. Ways for me to get my bearings, like the paths – ways for me to find my way back to Oakhome when I need to.

In a hazel above us, high on a forked branch, is a messy nest of twigs and leaves.

"Squirrel's nest," says Papa Herne, looking up. "It's called a drey."

My toes ache and my pulse quickens at the thought of how high it is.

"Dreys can look a lot like a rook

or magpie's nest. But you can tell the difference. Squirrels like to weave leaves into their nest, birds don't."

As I walk away, still carrying Papa Herne on his bird, something flashes in front of us: reddish brown fur, tufted ears, bushy tail.

The squirrel scampers across the forest floor and darts up the tree.

Papa Herne tells me that the leaves of sick trees turn brown before autumn, that willow bark or willow water is good for unwell animals.

I think about how fearless the squirrel was as it corkscrewed up the hazel, how much of the forest is off the ground. "I'd like to have another go at climbing," I say, "but like you said, try something smaller."

"Alright, I think I know just the tree." Papa Herne grabs his blackbird's saddle horn and snaps his reins. "Follow me!"

His blackbird shoots forward with a quick flick of its wings, then glides through the air along the path, before dropping with a sharp turn into a stand of silver birches.

"Hey, wait!" I say, but Papa Herne doesn't stop.

I race after him through the silver-white trees, wondering where he's going. I climb under and over

fallen stems, pick my way round
holly bushes.

I startle a robin. It rushes to
a branch and calls *tic-tic, tic-tic*.

I don't stop, trying to keep sight of Papa Herne's
blackbird. But it's too fast, flying further and further
away with every wingbeat.

Then they're out of sight.

I carry on running through the silver birches until
I reach a sunlit glade. Papa Herne's bird is there, sitting
in the sun. Papa Herne stands with his staff, looking
towards a gnarled old tree. I'd recognize the tree
anywhere – it's the one from the yard at Harklights. It's
still bent over like a broken-backed man. The tree looks
so much smaller now, surrounded by a circle of towering
trees. I guess this is what living all those years at
Harklights did to it.

Papa Herne raises his staff. A jet of green light shoots
forwards and bursts when it hits the trunk, then spreads
around the boughs and branches in a weaving, flickering
dance of light.

The old tree trembles, twists, turns and transforms
into Half Crown.

He's still missing part of his rack of antlers.

"Half Crown, it's good to have you back," I say, as he trots over. I stroke his muzzle. Here and there on his antlers are tiny green buds.

"Will the broken bit grow back?"

Papa Herne nods. "It'll take a while. Trees heal themselves – they grow new branches an' cover over old wounds with new bark." He pauses, then adds, "I thought, if you wanted, we could try again with climbing onto his back."

"Yes," I say. "Let's do it." I take a breath.

"You can do this," says Papa Herne. "You just need to take yer time."

We start again with handholds and footholds, this time looking for them on Half Crown. He stands there, patient, not moving as I test a foothold on his leg.

Papa Herne lands his blackbird on Half Crown's broken antler. "Yer okay if you fall off. The worst you'll get is a couple of bruises. It's not that bad."

Climbing onto Half Crown's back is like packing matchboxes. The more I practise, the better I get. I feel more confident with Papa Herne's encouragement. Eventually, I climb up as easily as a key winding a clock.

As we leave the silver birch glade on the back of Half Crown, I run a hand down his rough bark. I'll borrow him, I decide, when I rescue Petal. I just need to come up with a way of getting on the back of one of the steam lorries.

After Papa Herne finishes a story about sheltering from a storm in a badger burrow, the Hobs leave the fire circle and head to their nest-huts to sleep. Just as I'm settling by the fire, a rustling sound draws nearer and nearer to the clearing. As I sit up, Half Crown appears between two oaks, rolling a nest-hut with his wooden muzzle. This one is so big that I could fit in it.

"What is it?" I ask.

"Hope you like the hut. Make yerself at home," says Papa Herne. "This is what the Home Keepers have been busy making. They had help from squirrels collecting up twigs an' leaves. They're as hard-working as bees."

I grin, seeing leaves woven into the nest-home. No one has ever done anything like this for me.

Half Crown nudges the nest-hut to its final resting place close to the roots of a huge oak.

"An' those sparrows we saw helped too," adds Papa Herne.

I get up and go over to Half Crown. He nuzzles my hand.

"Thank you," I say, but there's an awkward feeling rising in my chest.

Papa Herne looks concerned. "Are you alright?"

I clear my throat. "I don't really know what a home is," I say quietly.

All of the model homes I made were empty inside. I only imagined what life would be like in them: a library, an astrologer's tower, a drawing room with long windows and cabinets filled with interesting things.

Papa Herne looks sad – his eyes are shining. "A home isn't just a place where yer keep yer things. It's where yer part of a family – where you feel loved, where you feel like you belong."

"I don't have any things. Just my clothes and boots. I don't even have my penknife any more."

There's a silence that stretches out. "Homes can take some time to grow," says Papa Herne, breaking it. "Take the blackbird. It takes two weeks to make its nest. I know we made you a nest in a couple of days, but maybe you should give yerself a while to settle in. Add some of the things that you like to it." He wipes his nose and smiles. "An' I know just the place to get them."

"Where you got the human things?"

"I'll take you there."

"Tomorrow?"

"Tomorrow's Quarter Day. We'll go soon."

I wonder what the place will be like. I picture an abandoned house somewhere in the heart of the forest. Walls covered in ivy, nestled in a tangle of trees. A hidden place away from the human world.

The nest-hut is more comfortable than I could ever imagine. The curved walls all around make me feel cosy, protected, a shell against the surrounding night. As I fall asleep with the dormice, I imagine who might have lived in the abandoned house. Maybe I'm not the first orphan to escape Harklights. Maybe someone else got away.

CHAPTER TEN

QUARTER DAY

We're having breakfast when the rise and fall of birdsong in the forest changes to sharp alarm calls. Just as Papa Herne puts his hat on, a blackbird comes racing into the clearing and lands roughly, Genna astride its back.

"What's happened?" says Papa Herne.

Genna looks pale as she climbs off. She mouths something, but the words don't come out.

A loud roar cuts the air. Genna's blackbird takes off without her. The others at the bird stable fly free.

My heart thuds wildly.

This is the Monster.

"Stag," says Papa Herne. "He's making a fighting call."

Nox frowns. "Can't be."

There's another angry roar, this time much closer. A hulking red-brown form moves between the trees, just outside the clearing, close to the Hob huts.

Papa Herne's right. As the stag lumbers into the clearing, we all freeze.

"Something's wrong," says Papa Herne. "He's s'posed to be friendly. Quick, everyone hide!"

The Hobs scatter, scurrying in all directions. Mama Herne grabs Linden. Nissa grabs Tiggs, who's holding Tuff. Genna carries a crying Tiya. Only Papa Herne, me and Nox stay where we are.

The stag is huge. Sharp pointed antlers. Powerful hooves. He eyes the Hobs, then charges at Finn, who's running to the huts.

Papa Herne casts about, looking for something.

"What are you doing?" yells Nox.

"It's okay, it's okay," says Papa Herne.

Finn backs up against the wall of one of the huts.

The stag swings his antlers at Finn. I flinch but he ducks. The antlers smash into the hut. Finn steps away, then easily slips into the gap between two huts.

"Hey! Over here!" I find myself shouting.

The stag turns around, bellows at us, then turns

back to look for Finn, smashing more of the Hob huts. Finn is too quick though – or lucky – and as the antlers crash into my hut, he escapes, sprinting to where some of the other Hobs are, beyond the clearing.

I breathe deeply. "That was close." I'm relieved Finn escaped but I can't help my eyes stinging. My hut is broken. I only just got it.

"Where's yer staff?" says Nox to Papa Herne.

Papa Herne stares at the mess of broken twigs and moss. "In my hut."

"We need a distraction," says Nox.

"I think we've got one," I say.

The stag growls, my hut impaled on its antlers. It thrashes its head wildly, trying to shake it off. The fur on its neck is wet – there's a dark blood stain.

I blink back tears and wonder if the stag got injured in a fight.

The stag roars again and lumbers forward, facing Papa Herne, me and Nox.

"You two distract him, I'll get the staff," cries Papa Herne.

Nox's eyes go wide. "Don't we have a better idea?"

Papa Herne shakes his head. "Not at the moment."

"Hey, let me down!" yells Nox as I pick him up.

"I can run faster," I say firmly, putting him in my shirt pocket.

The stag lowers his rack of antlers and roars at Papa Herne, who's creeping towards the broken nest-homes.

I wave my arms. "Over here!"

"Throw something at it," yells Nox. "Not me."

I pick up one of the sticks the Hobs were using as a fireside bench and throw it. The stag flinches as it glances off his wound, then bellows angrily and moves towards us.

"That's it, come on, come on," I murmur, stepping backwards.

As I step past the fire, I bend down to grab one of the larger part-burned sticks. It glows orange at the end.

"What are you doing?" says Nox. "We can't harm him – Forest Law!"

"How are we supposed to stop him then?"

"We just need to keep him distracted."

"What if Papa Herne doesn't find his staff?"

"Then we'll have to think of something else."

I step away to the edge of the clearing. The stag follows us, pacing faster, sniffing the air. I wonder if it's our breakfast he's smelling, or me.

I step out of the clearing and hide behind a tree. "What's taking Papa Herne so long?"

"I dunno," says Nox. "Let's go with the backup plan."

"What's that?"

"Run!"

I turn and run, following Fox Path, heading west. The stag charges behind us, head lowered. My hut is still tangled in his sharp antlers, making him look like some kind of tree-stag.

"Keep going!" calls Nox.

A surge of energy washes through me. My legs feel as if they are sprung clockwork and could run for hours.

But then something catches my foot – a rock. I lunge forward, hands outstretched to break my fall. Nox yells as I roll on my back to protect him.

Overhead, I glimpse Papa Herne on his blackbird, arcing between the trees.

He's got his staff!

Papa Herne raises it – a jet of green light shoots out.

Ivy on a nearby tree sends long tendrils racing across the forest floor. They slither and twist, coiling round the stag's legs, binding him tight.

Thud.

The stag drops heavily to the ground, inches from us, straining as the ivy winds round his body.

Papa Herne and his blackbird swoop round and land on the ground.

I drag huge gulps of air into my lungs. My heart drums. "That was close."

"Close?" cries Nox. "We nearly got killed! Put me down."

I lift Nox from my pocket and place him next to Papa Herne as he climbs down from his saddle. The Hob leader walks up to the stag and places a small hand on the beast's ivy-bound muzzle. The stag glares fiercely at us and makes a low growling sound.

"Easy, easy," says Papa Herne. "Wick, Nox, help me calm him."

Nox and I draw closer. The moment I lay my hands on the stag's muzzle, he writhes and squirms, trying to break free.

"Easy," says Papa Herne in a soothing voice. "If yer scared of him, it makes him scared."

I take a deep breath, feeling my hands grow warm against the fur. After a few minutes, the stag lets out a long breath and drops his head. I carefully pull away the tangle of moss, twigs and leaves from his antlers, all that's left of my broken hut. The sight of it brings back the ache of seeing my models burn.

"Right, let's have a look at that wound. Wick, could you lift me up?"

I lift Papa Herne and set him on the stag's red-brown shoulder. There's a hole, oozing blood.

"Bullet wound," I say, going cold. "Old Ma Bogey did this."

Apart from her crossbow and prized shotgun, I know she owns a six-shooter pistol.

"She's coming to get Wick. This is a warning," says Nox, fixing me with a hard stare. "Told you he would bring trouble."

A knot tightens in my stomach. What if Nox is right? What if she's in the forest now?

"It's not Wick's fault," says Papa Herne.

"But he's human! Humans are trouble!" There's anger in Nox's voice.

"That's enough!" cries Papa Herne. "Calm down!"

"Don't tell me to calm down!" hisses Nox.

The stag snorts and silences everyone.

"Look," says Papa Herne quietly. "We're all worked up about what just happened. But if we keep calm and work together, we can get through this."

Nox clenches his fists and looks as if he's about to say something, but he doesn't.

All the years I can remember, Old Ma Bogey has

stayed at Harklights and only left to go to town. The only hunting I've known her to do was to shoot the birds that dared to come and land in the yard, or on her roof. The knot in my stomach grows tighter.

My heart thuds.

What if she's changed her mind? And now she's decided to come to the forest with one of her guns?

I'm in danger – *everyone's* in danger.

Everything about this makes me afraid. Hobs and birds and wild animals could be targets. Has she shot other animals? Is that why the orphan cubs don't have mothers?

I don't know what to do – whether I should go looking for her or leave.

Papa Herne must know what I'm thinking because he says, "We don't know she's in the forest. Not yet anyways. We'll keep a watch out. She's not the only human with a gun."

I help Papa Herne gather medicine things from one of the wrecked huts. There's a pair of tweezers, a bundle of moss and spider's web. And there's a small bottle of propolis, a sticky dark-brown oil that bees make. Papa Herne is too small to use the tweezers, so I try. The bullet is buried deep. The stag tenses. Every time the tweezers scrape against the bullet, I want to be sick.

I hold my breath, clamp my jaw. Then I dig the tweezers in, ignoring the warm blood that's filling up the hole like a well.

As soon as the bullet's out, I drop it in my pocket. I'm going to take it back to Harklights. It doesn't belong in the forest.

Papa Herne plugs the wound with all the moss and spider's web – plus more moss that Nox and I gathered – then empties the whole bottle of propolis over it.

"What are we, er, going to do with him?" I whisper.

"Let him stay where he is," says Papa Herne.

"I'll get him some camomile an' arnica," says Nox. "He needs to sleep an' heal. You two go help the others." There's a long pause, as we all take stock of what's just happened. Then Nox looks at me in a way that he hasn't before. "Thank you for saving me an' digging the bullet out of the stag. Guess I were wrong about you – not all humans hurt."

All of the nest-huts that were on the ground are smashed to pieces. Some of the Hobs walk among them in a daze, rescuing what they can from the wreckage. Others sit crying, clinging to each other, hardly believing what has happened, taking shaky sips of dewdrops that Mama Herne and Nissa carry on leaves.

"Everything's broken," says Tiggs, wiping snot from his nose.

"We have nothing," says Linden, looking at the flattened hut he shared with Tiggs.

"We still have each other," says Finn, wrapping his arms round their shoulders. "At least no one got hurt."

Papa Herne picks up a twig then throws it down. "We can always rebuild our homes. Till then, the homeless can stay in bird nests an' by the fire."

"Wick's really good at building things," pipes up Nissa. "You should see the hut he made by the deer pond. He made it with sap an' twigs."

"It was nothing," I say. "I was just playing."

"No, it were brilliant. You should show the others."

I get up from the ground, rising above the Hobs, and head to the edge of the clearing.

"Where are you going?" hollers Papa Herne.

"To fetch the twig-hut," I say. This is a way I can make things right, I realize – show that I'm a human who makes things instead of destroying them.

On my way back to the deer pond, the rising and falling birdsong has returned and there's a bumbling hum of bees. But I feel my chest tighten.

Old Ma Bogey is coming. Shooting the stag was her calling card.

I keep expecting to meet her, stepping out from behind a tree. Pressing the cold circle of her pistol barrel against my neck.

Halfway to the deer pond, a jay swiftly takes to the air from a branch a little way ahead of me, calling out in alarm.

My scalp prickles. I stop, looking in all directions, trying to see what startled it.

There's no movement.

Must be Old Ma Bogey. She's waiting behind a tree.

The thought floods me with fear. My heart thuds fast in my ears and throat.

"I know you're there," I cry out.

I wait.

Nothing.

Then slowly, ahead of me, two pointed ears, orange-red, rise up from a patch of ferns into bright sunlight.

A fox.

The fear that it's Old Ma Bogey disappears. The fox pokes her head above the ferns. She isn't scared by my presence. She stays still, in the sun, silently watching me with  fire-coloured eyes. Then she raises her head, shows me her white throat and sniffs the air.

My breathing is too fast, too shallow. I take several deep breaths and blow them out, unwinding the tension I've been holding onto.

The fox watches me intently.

I stare back, marvelling at her colour, at how peaceful yet alert she is. She seems to draw on the calmness of the trees that surround us.

I don't know how long we stand there watching each other, breathing in the clean forest air. But it's enough for me to calm down. Close by the fox, I notice a tree with a wound that new bark has nearly covered up, just like Papa Herne taught me.

The fox's ears twist, hearing something I can't. Then she turns and melts into the ferns.

When I arrive at the deer pond, the twig-hut is exactly where I left it when I rushed to save Tiggs from the water. The place is deserted, except for the frogspawn and dragonflies flitting in wild angles over the water.

On my return walk, I realize that as long as I'm here, and Old Ma Bogey is looking for me, I'm putting the Hobs in danger. I realize for the first time that I need to do more than sneak back in the middle of the night and rescue Petal.

I need to confront Old Ma Bogey and stop her.

The idea seems too huge – impossible.

The palms of my hands break out in a sweat. My heart thuds as a breath catches in my throat.

I'm not ready. Not yet.

I force myself to take long breaths of clean forest air and be like the fox, drawing on the calmness of the trees that surround me. It works. I feel calmer and alert. I might not be ready now, but I will be. I'll get stronger, be stronger, here in the forest.

When I arrive at Oakhome, I put the twig-hut down in the clearing.

Papa Herne walks up to it. He runs his hands over the walls, looks up at the sloped roof and nods in approval. "This is good. D'you think you could build us more of these?"

I smile at the memory of my matchstick models. "Yes, but I'll need some help."

For a few minutes, I think about the old models I used to make. But then my thoughts turn. I can do better. Why make Hobs homes that look like miniature town houses? There's nothing like Hobs in the world – apart from wood sprites. They deserve something special. A different kind of home, something that's just for them.

CHAPTER ELEVEN

BLANKET OF STARS

With my heel, I clear a patch of ground where the old coals of the cooking fire sit, then smooth it down flat with my hand.

I take twigs and lay them out end to end. The Hobs gather round and watch me intently. I keep adding twigs, until I make the outline of a dome with a flat base. The shape is one of those beehives made from woven straw – only taller. I then add torn circles of dead leaves to show where the entrance could go and the windows on two floors.

When I've finished, Linden walks up and stands in the middle of the skep shape.

"I like it, but it's flat. It could do with walls."

Nissa laughs. "This isn't the hut, it's just a picture of it!"

"I knew that," says Linden, looking embarrassed. He folds his arms, shoving his hands under his armpits.

After lunch, we make a start. It's surprising how quickly the Hobs work. They don't really need me. Papa Herne and Genna call red squirrels and rabbits to help. This time it doesn't matter who are Forest Keepers or Home Keepers – apart from Mama Herne looking after Tiya, and Nox looking after the stag, everyone is working together.

Hob furniture is rescued from the ruined huts. Broken sticks are moved into a huge pile. Some of the Hobs make trips to gather pine sap, using the full-grown badgers to transport it in old tea caddies. Blue tits and sparrows fly off to gather more twigs.

It's great sharing my model-making skills and not having to keep them a secret any more. The Hobs have ideas too, for upper storeys and staircases, balconies and windows. And there are passages, beams and roofs to think about. Now it's not just my idea, but something we are all working on together, that belongs to all of us. A warm feeling wells up inside me. The first home starts to take shape.

"It's becoming real," says Papa Herne as he climbs a ladder made from a comb with broken teeth.

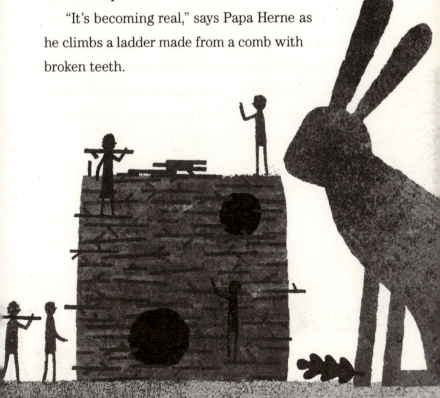

New beginnings and hope... I think back to one of the stories Petal told us years ago. It had been one of the worst days at the orphanage. Old Ma Bogey had lost her temper during Quota Inspection, smacking two of the orphans round the head so hard that they dropped to the floor. Then in the afternoon, when she caught them passing secret messages to each other, she threw them down the Well. That night, in the cold dark dormitory, amongst the tears, Petal told us about the Phoenix, the firebird that sang to the sun as it rose on the horizon every morning. When it got old, it burst into flame, burned itself up and was born again from its own ashes.

I tell Papa Herne the story as we glue pieces of the wall together.

"A story of hope," he says when I finish. "We all need those. The Phoenix bird sounds a lot like the sun. In midwinter, the sun goes down to its lowest point on the horizon, but it comes back again, rising up. It never really dies."

I dip another twig in the pine sap and press it against the row of others.

"Making these homes is a way of making new hope. Singing to the sun." Papa Herne adjusts his hat.

"Speaking of which…" He holds up a wooden loudhailer and turns to the other Hobs. "The Bring Forth party should have been today, but well – we shouldn't let things hold us back. Spring celebration is a time of new beginnings, new growth. We'll have the celebration tomorrow, just before sundown!"

The Hobs cheer.

Hearing Papa Herne talking about hope stirs courage in me. I breathe deeper, stand taller. The more I think about courage, the more I realize just how strong I already am. If I've been brave enough to escape from Old Ma Bogey – and face my fear of heights – then I'm ready to go back to Harklights. I don't want to wait for her to come and find me.

The Hobs whisper with excitement as they carry on building.

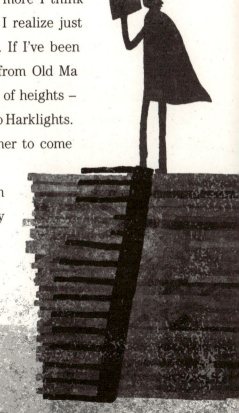

Tomorrow night. After the party. That's when I'll return. Half Crown will carry me back over the wall, when everyone is asleep. Somehow, some way, I'll get into the house, gather up Old Ma Bogey's guns and crossbow and beating stick and throw them down the Well. Then I'll find Petal. Part of me wants to bring all the orphans – except Padlock – to Oakhome. Papa Herne said he wanted to take them all when we escaped before, so maybe I can find a way to make it happen. I'm sure he'll be happy to see everyone, but I'm not sure what Nox will say.

Eventually the Hobs stop working and prepare dinner and feather beds for the night by the fire.

I sit with Nissa at the edge of the clearing. She's choosing small rocks for her catapult.

"The stag came from the North," she says. "Where the Monster comes from."

"I think I know who the Monster is," I say.

"Old Ma Bogey?"

"Yeah. She's got guns."

Nissa's eyes go wide. "How could I forget?"

"But if she's coming for me, then why was she in the North shooting a stag?"

She gives me a curious look. "What makes you think she's coming for you?"

"Because she takes things away from people. It's what she does. She doesn't want me to have anything, least of all a new home."

Nissa sets her jaw. "We can stop her. If she's not in the forest, we can go back to Harklights."

"It's dangerous."

"Course it's dangerous," says Nissa. "But it's dangerous doing nothing too."

My stomach is wound tight. I wonder if I should tell Nissa my plan. If I do, she'll want to come with me. I rub the back of my neck. "I don't know. Last time, I nearly got shot when I tried to get away from her. And Petal got caught. It's a bad idea." I say this as much to myself as to Nissa.

Nissa gives me a hard stare, then her eyes narrow. "There's something you're not telling me."

"Like what?"

"You're already planning to go back, aren't you?"

I look away. "I was, er, I'm just…" My words are hollow. It's obvious I'm hiding something.

"You're as bad as Papa Herne," says Nissa, sounding

wounded. "I thought you were my friend! You're supposed to tell me things, not hide things from me."

"I do tell you things. I…" I don't know what to say. Then the words come to me. "You're Papa Herne's daughter. What would he say if I let you come along and something happened?"

"I know I'm his daughter," says Nissa, raising her voice. "But that don't make me any different from anyone else or stop me wanting different things."

There's a growing silence between us.

"I know all about wanting different things," I say in a low voice. "Back at Harklights, it's what we all dreamed of. New parents. New home. New lives to live. You'd be brilliant if you came with me, but if something happened it'd cost me living with the Hobs…and I can't risk that."

Nissa sighs deeply. "Yer right." She rests her hand on the catapult tucked into her belt. "When are you going?"

"Tomorrow night." It feels strange hearing my thoughts turned into words. They feel more real.

"I don't like it." She sets her jaw again. "But I won't say anything to Papa."

170

After dinner, Papa Herne and I go out into the forest for a walk, carrying a human lantern the Hobs found. We head west, away from Oakhome along Hawk Path, into the lowering light. We're surrounded by the evening chorus – the *chook-chook-chook* and chirrup of blackbirds, the warble of a lone robin. The air is cool. Papa Herne stands in my sweater pocket, clutching the pocket edge as if it's a handrail. We pass the high ridge bank of birch trees and a tangle of overgrown brambles. My fear that Old Ma Bogey is coming hasn't gone away. It's still there, waiting for me in the quiet moments between words.

As we walk, Papa Herne points things out to me and tests me on my Forest Keeping. "What does a robin's distress call sound like?"

"Tic-tic."

"What d'you give a sick rabbit?"

"Willow bark or willow water."

"In which quarter of the forest are the warrens?"

"North-East."

"Yer doing very well," says Papa Herne. "One day, you'll know every inch of this forest."

I stare at the trees touched by lantern light.

"I'd like that," I say. I want to know everything about my new home.

Papa Herne touches the silver oak-leaf clasp of his cloak. "You'll be a great Forest Keeper like me an' protect the forest."

When it's dark, bats swoop in the air above us, drawn to the storm of insects circling the lantern. After a while, Papa Herne nods to one of the wooded slopes under the forest moon. We follow a winding path up through the trees to a tall rocky outcrop. The outcrop is a series of uneven boulders with flattened tops, each like a rough step on a giant's staircase.

I climb, making my way up slowly, placing the lantern in nooks that become handholds and footholds. I don't feel so afraid as I did up the tree – it's not a long way down to the next step.

Papa Herne says nothing, but I still hear his words of encouragement ringing through me.

When we reach the crest – a rock ledge like an upturned flat iron – we are nearly level with the surrounding treetops. Wooden towers, steeples and spires spread out in all directions.

There's a warm glow in my chest, like a second sun. "I couldn't have done this without you," I say.

"I did nothing," Papa Herne replies. "You did all the climbing."

I blow out the lantern and sit on the ledge under the blanket of stars. Their cold light blazes brightly, like glittering jewels. I know they're the same stars as the ones I saw at Harklights, but they seem brighter here, and there are more of them. I tilt my head back and wait to see if I can spot a falling star.

Hoo.

The low hoot breaks the silence. It comes from a cradle of branches close to us.

"It's alright," says Papa Herne from my shirt pocket. "She's one of the eagle owls. They can't talk of course, but they're great listeners. I come up here sometimes an' tell them the things on my mind."

The owl's head pivots towards us. Her eyes are huge dark pools that stare deep into mine. Something passes between us. I'm in awe, caught under her spell. Magic isn't just tiny babies, tree-stags and wood sprites. It's moments like this.

"Owls are night kings an' queens," says Papa Herne, "an' they're hunters."

The owl blinks and turns her head to study something on one of the lower branches.

Papa Herne clears his throat. "So, what d'you think of Havenwood Forest?"

"It's brilliant. These have been the best days of my life. The forest lessons, the climbing, the fireside stories. It feels as if I've been here for weeks and weeks."

"I'm glad you came to live with us. I wanted to show you what a family could be. Families aren't just blood, they're where the heart takes root."

Papa Herne's words thrum through me, doubling my happiness. He spreads his arms and gives me a hug. It's tiny, but just what I need.

After sitting for a while under the stars, Papa Herne says, "Best get back. We need to be up before sunrise."

"Why so early?" I reply.

"You never seen dawn in the forest. The tide of night turns, the sun rises an' washes over everything with its light."

I make the climb down inch by inch. It's easier this time, as if my hands and feet somehow recognize the rough edges of rock. The wild wonder of the owl still holds me and won't let go.

Everything is pink-grey and blue-grey in the early morning light. Even though it's before dawn, some of the birds are starting their chorus: blackbirds, song thrushes, robins and wrens. Papa Herne stands on Half Crown's antlers as we ride through the forest quietly listening. The air is still cool, but this time there's a thin mist weaving in and out of leaves.

As we approach an old oak, Papa Herne points up.

When he said the Hobs had found a human dwelling in the forest, I'd assumed it would be on the ground. I didn't expect it to be this – a cobbled-together treehouse, cradled in branches, a good fifteen feet or more off the ground. I remember my thought about another orphan escaping and staying in the forest.

"Did you ever see anyone?" I ask.

"No. It's always been empty. I think whoever stayed must have left a long time ago."

I climb down from Half Crown and walk closer to get a better look. The treehouse has different sized windows that look as if they've come from barns, huts, tool sheds and shacks. Each of them is shut. The old door set into one side is open and there's a small balcony and a rope ladder hanging down, not to the ground, but close to some of the lower branches. On a sign near the door are large printed letters:

I walk right up to the oak. "This is where you got the human things, isn't it?"

"Yeah. D'you want to use the ivy to help you climb up?" asks Papa Herne as I put him down on an old stump.

"No, I'll be fine." But a wave of fear rushes through me as I stand by the trunk.

"Go slowly," says Papa Herne. "Take yer time. Find a hold an' test it. Remember to breathe."

At Harklights, everything was fast-paced, working in rhythm to the speed of the Machine. A race against time. Here, the forest has a different rhythm. I follow Papa Herne's instructions. Even though my heart is thumping, it's with excitement as much as fear. I've never felt so alive.

I climb slowly, finding nubs of bark and knotholes to help me. In the forest, I can be another Wick, a new Wick, a better version of myself. Someone who opens up to his friends. Someone who's not afraid of heights.

Papa Herne calls up through his wooden loudhailer. "You can do it. Go easy."

I take strength from his voice.

This time, I don't slip. Each step I take, I'm sure of my holds.

I reach the ladder and climb its rungs to the wooden platform. I steady myself and glance down at the forest floor below. That warm blaze of achievement engulfs me again, filling me with a glow. It feels as if I've unlocked something inside myself. I look out at all the trees I'm ready to climb, all the trees that are waiting just for me. Now it feels as if there's no place in the forest I can't go.

"I can see why you do this," I call down.

"Why's that?" asks Papa Herne.

I take a deep breath. "Because it makes you feel like a giant. Like you could take on anything."

"Go in, have a look round. We'll wait here!"

My heart thuds as I step inside. The treehouse is a single dusty room. A table stands in the middle, surrounded by tea-chest seats. At one end of the room, a thin curtain hangs down. At the other is a chipped washstand and a small stove.

The floor is littered with old dry leaves and bird mess. Lots of bird mess. Papa Herne is right – it doesn't look as if anyone has been here in years.

As I cross the room, the floorboards creak. Propped up on the small table is a tent of folded notepaper.

A note. With my name on it. *Wick*. Small, careful letters written in ink.

I wonder how long it's been there and who left it.

I pick it up. My fingers are as steady as a well-trained packsmith, but inside I'm trembling.

I open the note.

Knew you
could do it

— Papa Herne

I close the note with a huge grin on my face. I wonder when he came to put it up here. The grin fades as I notice an empty box of buckshot cartridges. Close by, under a tin of pipe-leaf, is a black leather-bound notebook.

It's empty, except for a third-class ticket for the Liverpool and Manchester Railway. Next to it is a copy of *The Empire Times*. It's old. From twelve years ago. I flick through the pages. One of the advertisements catches my eye. It's full-page. My reading skills are rusty so I go over the words slowly:

HARKLIGHTS PATENT EVERSTRIKES
BRINGING LIGHT TO ALL YOUR FAMILY
USED BY HIS MAJESTY THE KING

There's an etching of a family – father, mother, son, daughter – in a drawing room with comfy chairs arranged around a huge fireplace. The son is crouched forward, lighting a neat stack of logs and twisted paper with an Everstrikes match. His father, who looks to be an older version of him, crouches by his side, an encouraging arm around his shoulder. The mother and daughter sit in the chairs and hold their hands up, clapping with delight. Everyone is smiling and there's light in their eyes. The boy's smile is broadest. It looks as if he's proud to be the one lighting the fire for everyone.

On the hearthrug by his feet is a long fork resting on a plate piled with crumpets.

My stomach feels tight, as if it's trying to keep hold of all my feelings and stop them escaping.

This is what people think of when they see Harklights? Happy families?

I close the newspaper quickly, trying hard to pretend I've not seen the advertisement. It doesn't work. I can't shake the picture. Do my parents ever think of me at Harklights? Or did they forget I was ever abandoned? Do they hold new children in their hearts now, and light fires with them in a new home?

At the back of the treehouse, behind the thin curtain, are a couple of low bunks with overhead cupboards. There's a trunk on the floor nearby with an open lid. Inside are some clothes: white collarless shirts, a cotton scarf, pairs of stovepipe trousers. As with the sweater, the clothes are a bit too big for me right now, but they're things I could grow into. I hold up one of the shirts. There's a shirt pocket to carry Hobs in, but some of the buttons are missing. Genna must have taken them as treasure for Tiggs.

In one of the cupboards I find stacks of tins, thirty

or more. All of them filled with peaches. I take out four and chuck them in a leather haversack I find, along with the notebook, some of the clothes and a tin-opener from the kitchen area.

There's a steep ladder leaning, unfixed, against the back wall. I climb it cautiously, heart fluttering, and step out onto the roof. I keep away from the edge as it's a long way down. From here, the whole forest stretches in all directions. To the north is open heath and, beyond, a ridge of tree-covered hills. To the west are mountains.

In the east, the sun rises at the edge of the sky. The first rays catch the treetops, crowning them in glowing gold. A thin column of dirty grey smoke winds into the air.

Harklights.

My stomach sinks. It's not that far.

I can't see the factory or the chimney, but the smoke is enough to start the roar and rumble of the Machine in my head again.

CHAPTER TWELVE
BRING FORTH

As Papa Herne and I return to Oakhome, the image of the grey smoke of Harklights shadows my thoughts. If the Machine is on, then the orphans must be working already. We never start work this early. Something must have happened. Is this a punishment for something? My jaw tenses.

I was right. It has to be tonight. It's time I stopped her.

I turn the plan over in my mind. I'll climb the wall of the orphanage and find an open window. And if there's not one, then I'll climb up onto the roof and wrench off the roof tiles – make my own window. We'll rescue Petal *and* the other orphans. And if Old Ma Bogey wakes up and I see her, I'll tell her she needs to invent a new Machine that doesn't need orphan workers, not waste her time making stupid mechanical beetle toys. And if she tries to stop us or threatens us with her shotgun again, I'll tell her I'll come back with a gang of wild animals and let them run riot through the house and factory.

I must be tense because Papa Herne turns around on the palm of my hand and says, "Are you alright? What is it?"

"Nothing."

I don't want any of the Hobs to get hurt. I've put them in enough danger as it is. Luckily no one got hurt when the stag destroyed Oakhome. I can't risk anything happening to them again.

I take a deep breath and let it out slowly. "Actually, I was thinking I could climb some more trees on the way back."

Papa Herne raises an eyebrow. "How many were you thinking of?"

I shrug. "How long have we got?"

Everyone joins in with the preparations for the Bring Forth celebrations that mark the beginning of spring. Nox and Genna lead mouse-drawn carts packed with planted bluebells, primroses and snowdrops, parking them alongside the clearing. Carts filled only with soil stand either side of the half-built house. Others arrive, laden with honey cakes, seed bread, sweet violet flowers, sorrel leaves, daisies, birch water and birch syrup.

A group of Home Keepers arrange the food on Hob-tables and a slate for me. Nissa puts out small jars filled with fireflies. I help Papa Herne hang long banners between the trees. The banners are decorated with the same design: blue-black silhouetted trees with weaving branches, on which sit all manner of forest animals and birds. When the decorations are finished, Oakhome looks beautiful. Everything is bathed in the evening sun. The leaves on the trees catch the light, shining with molten gold.

While the Hobs go and change into their party clothes, butterflies arrive and settle on the oaks around the grove. There are hundreds of them, closed-winged, showing their bark-brown colours.

I go through my rescue plan again and again in my head. I feel my muscles tighten. I can do this.

Then the Hobs gather round the half-built house.

All of them are wearing bright green. Even Baby Tiya has a leaf-green outfit.

I feel a bit left out. I don't have anything to change into. I only have my drab grey clothes.

A hush falls as Half Crown trots into the clearing and stops by the house's balcony, where all of the Forest Keepers stand. He lowers his head so Papa Herne can climb onto his muzzle. As Half Crown raises his head, Papa Herne calls out, "Before we begin our celebrations, I have a small announcement to make. Wick, as you know, has been living with us an' he's been training to be a Forest Keeper. Not only did he save Tiggs from drowning—"

"An' Tuff," pipes up Tiggs.

"That's right, an' Tuff." Papa Herne smiles. "An' he also saved Finn an' Nox from a wounded stag. He's got great patrol skills an' he's helping us rebuild our homes. He's still got more Keeper things to learn, but he's already proved he's made of the right stuff. An' he's conquered his fear of heights. He climbed *four* trees this morning."

A flush of pride runs through me. I'd have climbed twice that if we'd had time.

There's a round of clapping.

"An' so, it's time for Wick to get his cloak. Kneel, Wick," he adds in a solemn voice.

I'm not expecting this. I feel weightless. Breathless.

Just then, a flock of blue tits and sparrows carry a cloak through the air. It's not a patchwork of different fabrics like my other clothes, but a single cloak, dyed the same green as the others. The birds lower and hover in the air, then drop it onto my shoulders. This is more than I could ever hope for. I might have lived all my life at Harklights, but I belong with the Hobs now.

CHAPTER THIRTEEN

THE WHITE STONES

"This robe is the Cloak of the Forest," Papa Herne calls out. "May the forest offer you shelter, as you shelter an' protect the forest an' all its creatures."

Already I feel different. The cloak feels reassuring, like warm sun on my shoulders. I don't want to ever take it off.

"How did you make the cloak so fast?" I find myself asking. From the stitching, it looks as if it must have taken months.

Papa Herne gives me a knowing smile. "A question for another time."

Half Crown trots closer and lowers his wooden head. Sunlight glints off a silver leaf clasp in his mouth, larger than the ones the other Forest Keepers wear.

The clasp is handsome. Finely crafted. A burst of

warmth spreads through my chest. I feel complete. Old Ma Bogey was wrong when she said nobody wanted orphans because we were broken.

"You'll have to take it an' fix it to yer cloak," says Papa Herne in a low voice, before raising it again. "By the Four Corners of the Forest an' with this silver leaf clasp, I charge you with the title Forest Keeper."

He waits till I fasten my cloak, then adds, "Rise, Wick."

Feeling a tingle rush down my spine, I stand and face the crowd of Hobs. There's an explosion of cheering and clapping. I'm part of the Hob tribe now. I want to carry this moment for ever.

The other Forest Keepers join in with clapping. I give them a thumbs up.

Then Papa Herne taps his staff and raises his hands. "Let the Bring Forth celebrations begin!" Green light shimmers and shines, and ferns rise from the soil-filled carts by the half-built house. Their leaves are coiled, like watch-springs. Then they unfurl themselves slowly, making green arches.

All at once, the butterflies rise up, circling in the air. Flashing colours. Flickering wings, fluttering upwards.

The Hobs gasp at the orange-reds, brown-reds, yellows and blues. The hairs on my arms prickle. I think the colour will stay in my eyes for days.

"They're like…flying flowers," I murmur, watching the last of the butterflies drift away above the treetops.

As the sun goes down and the light fades, I sit and make small talk as a procession of Hobs comes and congratulates me. I don't see Nox and wonder if he's avoiding me.

"Well done," says Wyn, one of the Hobs who tends the fire.

"Thanks," I say distractedly, looking around.

Then I spot Nox – he's talking with Mama Herne. She's wearing a new dress she's sewn. From where I'm standing I can't hear their conversation, but Mama Herne is talking animatedly. Then she turns and goes off, leaving Nox standing on his own. There's a strange expression on his face, as if he's lost something and found something he didn't want at the same time. Maybe he's thinking about his wife. I wonder whether I should go over and talk to him.

"Well done, Wick."

I look down. It's Nissa, standing rigid. Her wild hair is still tangled, but she's wearing a cape made of flower petals.

"Thanks," I say.

She presses her lips flat. Her cheeks burn.

I feel awkward. I can tell that she wishes she was sitting where I am now, or next to me, wearing the same cloak of green. I wish that too. "You should be a Forest Keeper," I say. "You know more about the forest than I do. I haven't been here that long."

"Yeah, but it's what yer done that counts. You helped stop an' heal the stag." Her voice sounds strangled, tight.

I clear my throat. "Thanks for making me show my twig model to the others."

Nissa's smile flickers. "Yeah, well, if you have the knack for doing something, you should share it."

It doesn't feel right that Nissa isn't a Forest Keeper. When I'm back from Harklights with Petal and the others, I'll ask Papa Herne if he can train her.

"Wick! Wick! Congratulations!"

Linden and Tiggs come running over. Tiggs has Tuff with him.

"Yer a hero!" says Linden.

Tiggs looks up at me. "I want to be a Forest Keeper just like you."

"Maybe one day you will be," I say.

"You can teach me about looking after the animals an' everything."

I smile. "Can you excuse me? There's someone I need to speak to…"

But when I look up, Nox has gone.

I stare at the empty space where Nox had been standing. I was hoping he would congratulate me. I know we aren't exactly friends, but I thought things were different now. Or was he just pretending, to make Papa Herne happy? My heart sinks. Maybe in his eyes, the cloak and silver leaf don't mean anything. Maybe in his eyes, I'm always going to be the human boy, and I'll never belong. All I want is to be accepted by all of the Hobs.

As it starts to get dark, the fireflies light up in the jars and the fire is lit. Music starts up. A band of Hobs play pipes, wood blocks and wood drums. The sight of piled food on my slate makes me realize I've not eaten since breakfast, but I'm not hungry. I pick up a small seed loaf topped with birch syrup but I can't eat. I'm tightly wound with the fear and excitement of going back to Harklights.

I get to my feet. I need to talk with Nox. I can tell him I know what it's like to feel alone even though you have lots of people around you. But as I make my way through the celebrating Hobs, a voice cries out.

"Hey, where d'you think yer going?" It's Papa Herne. "You need to dance."

"I was just…"

Papa Herne's eyes and face are shiny from sap wine. "Come on, you. Fire dance. This party is as much for you as it is for Bring Forth."

Papa Herne is right. This is for me. It feels amazing. My heart thrums with happiness. I was just another cog in the Machine. But now I'm forest-shaped – my life revolves around the forest and all who live here.

I'm wondering how I can join in without stepping on

anyone when Mama Herne appears and pulls Papa Herne away to dance. I take my chance and slip away.

Nox is over by the edge of the circle of oaks, standing in the firelight under one of the large banners. He's up to something. He's just as I was when I was at Harklights, trying not to be noticed. He glances all round to see if anyone is watching. Then he steps back into the shadows.

Instinctively I hide behind one of the oaks and peer round it to watch him.

Nox walks away from the sound of music and laughter and heads west along Fox Path. He takes a flat leaf from his cloak and blows on it, making a shrill whistle.

I wait for the Milk Hare to come, but a badger appears instead, shuffling along, snout low, nosing the ground. When the badger reaches Nox, it stops and waits for him to walk up its black-and-white snout and take a seat. Once Nox is settled, the badger trundles off into the South-West Quarter.

I follow them, keeping my distance.

We pass Bramble Patch and the Claw Tree, which the badgers use to sharpen their claws. After a while, Nox and the badger reach a cluster of birch trees, their tangle of exposed roots knitted and fused into a sloped bank.

It's not somewhere I've been before.

Nox walks back down the length of the badger's snout, steps off, then climbs the bank and stops.

I'm startled when he slips through a gap between the roots.

Where's he going?

None of the gaps are big enough for me to fit through, so I climb to the top of the bank and clamber over the knitted roots. Here the slope drops into a deep ravine. There's no moss, only mouldering wood, decaying leaves and the damp smell of these things. It's as if the sun never reaches into this rift in the earth. It takes a few moments for my eyes to adjust to the gloom and see Nox. He descends a flight of Hob-sized stone steps and takes a turn through a tiny stone arch resting on two pillars.

I didn't know this place existed.

"Nox, wait..." I whisper, but he ignores me or can't hear me.

The steps are too small for me. I climb down into the ravine, careful that I don't slip on the wet tree roots. "Nox..."

I've lost him.

I step over the arch then follow the stone path as it descends into a deep sunken lane, high-sided with black earth and filled with a low mist. I hug myself. The air down here is cold. A deep chill cuts through my Forest Keeper cloak.

After a few minutes, I catch sight of Nox again. He stops at the end of the misty lane, where the broken roots of a fallen tree and hard-packed earth make a wall. Beneath the wall are dozens and dozens of white stones, like large teeth.

Nox kneels before a group of three white stones and bows his head.

A shiver runs through me. "It's a graveyard," I say. "I never realized..."

"You shouldn't be here," replies Nox in a sharp tone.

I glance, stunned by the gravestones, which glow in the half-light. Three names: Willow, Bud and Twig.

"Who are they?"

Nox lets out a long sigh and his shoulders drop. "My wife an' my two children."

His words knock my thoughts sideways. "I'm sorry."

"I'm sorry too," says Nox with sadness in his voice.

I gasp and look around at all the stones. "There are so many. I thought the other Hobs—"

"Disappeared?" offers Nox. "Yeah, that's what everyone thinks, apart from me, Genna, Papa Herne an' Mama Herne."

My head reels. "The Monster. Nissa heard you and Papa Herne talking about it, but he said it was nothing."

"He wanted – *we* wanted – to protect everyone from the truth."

"But why?"

"We thought it were better if everyone thought their family in the other villages had just left their homes, gone somewhere else. Finn lost his parents, his brothers an' their families. Genna an' the children are all he's got. Many of us lost friends an' family."

It feels as if the ground is moving and staying still at the same time.

Nox dips his head. "Willow were out with our boys

on a picnic close by Owls Hatch... Nissa were good friends with my sons. They were the same age. They grew up together from acorn-cradle."

"The same age..." I'm dizzy, breathless.

"How could we tell her that the Monster took them away? It devoured everything. Birds, animals, plants, trees. All that stood in the path of its hunger an' terror..." He pulls out a folded piece of oil cloth and opens it, revealing a painted image of a dragon's head with a long snout.

"Nissa and I, we thought the Monster was Old Ma Bogey."

"It's much worse – something from a nightmare. Three times the size of a stag. Red scaly body. Huge claws. A ferocious jaw filled with teeth. Genna saw it. It's what stopped her talking. After the other villages were destroyed, the Monster stayed in Sixways Wood. We thought everyone would be safe if they kept away from the North..."

I catch sight of a silver leaf sat atop one of the white stones.

I'm struck with sadness, circled by fear. All those Hobs and animals and birds killed by the Monster.

And it's still out there.

"But it got closer. Now it roams Wayland Heath, past Lightning Rock. An' these last days, it's twice ventured into the edge of the forest. It's looking for more food. It's still hungry." Nox looks at me. His eyes are like black stars in the dark. "Everyone's safe in Oakhome as long as it stays away from us."

"There must be a way to stop it." I want to be able to do something, but I don't know what.

"I don't know. Promise me you won't tell Papa Herne about our talk."

"Why not?" I clutch onto the broken roots for support.

"You'll only stir up a hornet's nest of trouble." Nox scratches away the dead leaves from around his wife and sons' gravestones. Then he straightens up and wipes his hands together. "Well, we should be getting back. We don't want anyone to see you've gone...it's yer party you know."

I grit my teeth, scrunch my fists. Then I chase away an unwanted tear with the back of my hand.

I thought life in the forest would be safe. A sheltered place surrounded by trees. But it's not. It's like Harklights, only a different kind of dangerous.

As we turn to leave, a thin stream of soil falls from above our heads.

"What were that?" says Nox.

I strain to see in the darkness. Leaves move, as if somebody was just there.

CHAPTER FOURTEEN
THE DRAGON

Nox was right to say we should go back when he did. The party is in the last stages of winding down when we arrive back. There are only a dozen or so Hobs left talking, while foxes and mice pick at the leftover food. Mama Herne is putting the younger Hobs to bed. She finds me to say goodnight to them.

"Wick is gonna protect the forest now," says Mama Herne.

I smile at Linden and Tiggs, but my stomach sinks. How can I protect it – and them – against a monster? Mama Herne knows the truth about the Hobs who were killed – what does she really think I can do to stop it happening again?

I don't know how I feel. Nox told me not to say anything to Papa Herne, but I want to talk to someone.

"Where's Nissa?" I ask Mama Herne, keeping the need out of my voice.

"Oh, she's gone to her bed in the half-built home. Weren't feeling too well, poor thing. She said to say goodnight. Are you alright?"

"I'm fine. I wanted to talk to her, but it can wait."

Everything has changed now I know the truth about the Monster. I can't go back for Petal and the others, not just yet. I can't bring them here – it's not safe.

I watch as Mama Herne settles Linden and Tiggs in their feather beds.

The Hobs are in danger. I have to find out if there's anything I can do to help them, to stop this Monster. I'll find Nissa first thing in the morning, tell her everything Nox said. Then we'll both speak with Papa Herne. It's the only way.

It's not long before the music stops and the rest of the Hobs head off for bed. A group of Hobs gather light, collecting up the firefly lanterns and loading them onto a little cart.

The cart is filled with pine sprigs, which the fireflies love – it sends them crawling over and under each other, weaving invisible lines.

It's strange watching Papa Herne's contentment as he glances up at the hanging banners. Underneath his calm exterior is a terrible truth, locked away. The Monster is real. And it can kill.

"Goodnight, Forest Keeper," he says, heading to bed. "Don't stay up too late."

As the fire dies down, I spread the hot coals, making a fiery constellation that glistens and winks. I take off my cloak for the first time and lie down under my blanket.

It takes ages to get to sleep. My head swims with images. Clusters of flowers and dead badgers and dead foxes. A red dragon crunches Hobs as if they're acorns. Then I'm stuck on a carousel of trees, clambering over and under branches, trying to outrun the dragon…

I wake to overcast skies. Everything looks grey. All the colour has drained from the forest. Papa Herne and Nox are talking together as I climb out of my blanket and brush the dry leaves from my cloak.

"Morning, Wick," says Papa Herne. "How's our new Forest Keeper?"

"Good." My mind flits back to everything Nox told me last night.

Nox doesn't say anything, but he gives me a knowing nod.

Papa Herne tips his hat. "After breakfast, I thought we could go down to the South-East Quarter. See how the pine martens are doing."

"Great," I say, keeping a light tone in my voice. "But first I need to speak with Nissa."

Just then, Mama Herne comes running from the unfinished twig house with a folded piece of birch-paper that's nearly half her size. "Papa Herne! Quick!"

"What's wrong?" says Papa Herne.

"Nissa – she's gone."

Papa Herne's eyes widen with panic. "Gone where?"

"I found *this* on her bed." Mama Herne unfolds the birch-paper. There's a message written in blackberry ink.

Papa Herne reads the scrawled handwriting and covers his mouth. "No, no, no…"

I glance down at the note:

> Gone beyond Lightning Rock to fight
> the Monster with Genna's blackbird and
> a hawthorn spear.
> Wick is not the only one who can be
> a Forest Keeper. I can too.
>   Nissa

Nox fixes me with his eyes. "Guess she were there last night." Then he glances at Papa Herne. "I told Wick everything; he knows. He followed me to the graveyard."

"What! We said we weren't gonna—" Papa Herne cuts himself off as the weight of Nissa's words sink in. "We got to go after her – NOW."

My heart pounds. My mouth is dry. "How long has she been gone?"

"I don't know. She could be half-a-way across the forest by now."

I have a horrible sinking feeling. What if Nissa has already found the Monster? A tiny spear won't do anything. She doesn't stand a chance.

When we reach the bird hangar, Papa Herne and Nox jump off my hand and climb onto their blackbirds. They launch into the air and hover by my shoulder. I run from the clearing to where Half Crown waits and climb up onto his back. Then I cluck my tongue and dig my heels into his sides. "Come on, Half Crown."

I try to push bad thoughts away – try to focus on hope, and finding Nissa alright – but they crowd round me.

We race away through the trees. Branches whip past as I cling, tight-knuckled, to Half Crown's bark mane. The blackbird riders fly overhead.

There's a familiar knot in my stomach. It's my fault. If Papa Herne had trained Nissa instead of me, this wouldn't be happening. How does Nissa think she can fight it? What if she's dead? I feel cold, as if I'm back in the Hob graveyard.

Papa Herne and Nox scour the forest ahead in silence.

At the edge of the forest, we pass a place called Grey Lake, which has high cliffs on three sides and is squared by a beach. Beyond this is Wayland Heath with its patches of woodland and heather and open spaces.

It takes nearly half an hour to reach Lightning Rock – a huge grey-black outcrop with a jagged split through the middle. Somewhere beyond here is where the Monster roams. I dig my heels into Half Crown's flanks and tug on his mane. As he slows to a trot, Papa Herne's and Nox's blackbirds swoop through the gap in the rock. It's like a canyon to the Hobs, but still wide enough for a tree-stag.

"Nissa!" cries Papa Herne.

"WAIT!" roars Nox. "It's dangerous – the Monster could be anywhere."

I push Half Crown forward through the canyon. Ahead is another blackbird in flight, a rider between its wings. They hold tight to what looks like a tiny spear.

It's Nissa. We made it in time. She hadn't been gone for long.

I want to let out a wild cry of relief.

But Nissa isn't stopping. Her blackbird races through the air, weaving over and under branches. As Papa Herne and Nox close in, Nissa's blackbird drops, corkscrewing in a steep dive into the hollow trunk of a huge fallen oak.

There's no way Half Crown can follow, so I steer him round the hollow oak and break into a gallop. I catch a glimpse of Nissa's blackbird through a broken section of trunk, then push on, faster. We leap over a tangle of fallen branches. At the other end of the trunk, I pull the tree-stag to a halt, then jump off.

I wait by the tree hollow.

There's a flash of brown-grey. Nissa drops the Hawthorn spear as her blackbird crashes into me. Then Nissa flips and somersaults through the air—

I dive and catch her before she hits the ground, cupping her in my hands like a fragile egg.

"What are you doing?" she cries, as I place her carefully on the ground. Her face is pinched in annoyance. "You could have *killed* me! And look what you did to my bird! Sometimes I wish you'd never come to the forest!"

The words bite, but I say nothing. Nissa's blackbird lies on the ground nearby, unconscious.

"I don't need yer help!" she yells, picking up the spear again. "I can do this on my own! I'm gonna stab this into the Monster's foot. Then it'll stop attacking as it'll be in too much pain. Then we can take the thorn out again and it'll be friendly, like what happened with the stag."

I can't see this ending well. "But the thorn might make the Monster attack even more."

"You don't know that!" she fires back.

Papa Herne's and Nox's blackbirds drop from the air and land as Nissa storms off.

"Nissa – wait!" cries Papa Herne. "I'm sorry for not telling you about the Monster."

Nissa stops in her tracks and turns around. "You should have told me. I'm not a child, I'm old enough to know. And why didn't you take me to see

214

the wood sprites? You took Wick!"

"I did take you," says Papa Herne. "When you were still in the acorn-cradle. The sprites saw yer future. They told me you would be a Forest Keeper – one of the greatest. You would follow the Forest Law an' protect it." His voice falters. "But they said there would be a monster that would come twice. An' when it came a second time, you would find out an' go after it, an' you'd be…"

Nissa stares at Papa Herne, thunderstruck. "You should have told me what the sprites said," she says in a wounded voice. "I would have understood. Even though I…" Her shoulders slump.

She drops her hawthorn spear.

My heart tightens as Papa Herne walks towards her. "I wanted to keep you safe, that's why yer a Home Keeper."

Tears trickle down Nissa's cheeks. "Oh, Papa."

Papa Herne pulls Nissa into an embrace. "I'll begin yer training next solstice, if that's what you want."

"What's the *point*?" she says in a clotted voice. "How are we gonna protect the forest if we don't fight the Monster?"

Papa Herne blinks as she buries her face in his shoulder.

Nox drops his head.

"I'm sorry, Wick," says Papa Herne. "I should have told you about the Monster too… I should have told everyone in Oakhome. I thought I could protect you from the truth. It were a mistake."

Nissa peers up at me. "Thanks for coming after me. An' I didn't mean what I said about—"

"I know," I cut in.

A heavy, low thudding sounds in the distance.

Nissa's eyes grow wide. "Is that the Monster?"

"Yeah." Nox stares down the canyon in terror.

None of us can see anything but trees.

"What are we gonna do?" says Nissa.

The thudding grows louder. Nearer.

"Leave it be," replies Papa Herne. "We can't fight it. An' if it comes anywhere near Oakhome, we'll move everyone south."

Nissa's blackbird comes round, hops to its feet and shivers its wings. Nissa looks defeated. She doesn't pick up the thorn spear again. All her strength and fight has gone.

The Hobs climb onto their birds and flee into the air. Papa Herne's bird swoops close to me. "Wick, come on, we got to get out of here!" Then he turns south and heads back towards Lightning Rock.

I tense as the ground trembles.

How big is this Monster?

I'm in two minds. Part of me wants to escape with the others. But I need to see what killed the Hobs, what threatens their home. I need to see if there's anything I can do to protect them and make the forest safe for both them and for the orphans – if I'm ever going to rescue Petal and the others.

I climb easily onto Half Crown's back. We hide behind a tree.

A bestial roar pierces the air, loud and close. It sounds metallic, as if the dragon has swallowed all the knights that came to battle it and has a bellyful of armour.

Three shapes burst through the trees. I freeze, but it's only a trio of deer racing away in panic. Half Crown lifts his head and watches the flash of their white tails.

"Not yet, Half Crown," I say.

The tree shakes as the footfalls of the Monster grow closer. An old bird nest trembles, then falls from a branch above us and drops to the ground.

I get a glimpse of the Monster through the trees.

Nox wasn't wrong about the size. Half as high as a tree, stout legs thicker than a trunk. As it lumbers towards us, I catch sight of something that looks like a humpback… No, it's a driver's cabin.

I gasp. The Monster isn't real. It's a machine…

But not like anything I've seen in newspaper pictures.

There's the faint shape of the driver sitting in the driving seat. The Monster reaches out with thick metal arms. An iron pincer-claw grabs hold of a tree. A spinning saw blade settles against the trunk, high up.

There's a whining sound, a turkey tail of sawdust.

The crown of the tree falls to the ground. The saw blade moves away and comes back lower, whirring through the base of the trunk. Then the topped-and-tailed tree is raised up into the air and lowered into a cradle on the Monster's back.

Then it hits me. The Monster – it's harvesting the trees.

With that tree gone, I get a clearer view. The Monster looks like something between a steam tractor, a lorry and one of Old Ma Bogey's mechanical beetles. Ferocious teeth form a painted snarl on the front.

The mechanical beetles aren't toys, they're models.

Behind the Monster is a wasteland. The forest is gone. All that's left are tree stumps, scrub and sawdust, and the long scars made by iron wheels. I know now why Papa Herne and Nox wanted to keep this a secret from the others. The horror would be too much.

Half Crown skitters nervously as the Monster passes by us.

Then I see it. Stamped metal letters on the side of the Monster:

TIMBER GOLIATH No.1

There's smaller lettering underneath. I squint to read it.

HARKLIGHTS LOGGING COMPANY
A DIVISION OF HARKLIGHTS MATCHES

My heart sinks. I feel sick.

Old Ma Bogey's matchwood.

I clap my hand over my mouth.

All of the trees she uses are from these woods and forests. The homes of Hobs, animals and birds, brought to Harklights to be cut, little by little, into matches. Packed into matchboxes by orphans who have no home.

I don't know why I never thought of this before, but now it's clear.

I see the truth. And I can't unsee it.

Half Crown and I race away.

When we reach Lightning Rock, the three bird-riders are waiting with horrified faces.

Papa Herne breathes a sigh of relief. "Thank the forest we all got away in one piece."

In the distance, the rhythmic footfalls of the Monster continue. But knowing it's a machine somehow makes it seem less of a threat.

"Did you see it?" says Papa Herne.

"Yes," I reply. "But it's not what you think."

"What d'you mean?"

"It's a machine. It needs someone to operate it. Do you

remember when we first met? Old Ma Bogey tried to shoot you."

Papa Herne nods. "I remember."

"The Monster belongs to her."

CHAPTER FIFTEEN

THE LEAF TRAP

"I'm going back," I say.

"But the Monster…" breathes Papa Herne. "It can't be stopped. I've tried."

I glance down at the carpet of leaves on the forest floor. I remember what Papa Herne said about stepping on hidden rabbit holes. It sparks an idea. "I know how we can stop it."

"How?" says Papa Herne.

"Tell us!" demands Nissa.

Half Crown raises his head in the direction of the Monster. His bark ears are pricked forwards. I pat his broad neck. "Leaves. We're going to need lots and lots of leaves. And your bird friends."

The Hobs look at me with confusion. I quickly tell them my idea and watch as it catches alight in their minds, igniting smiles, which spread to their eyes.

Then I race north with Half Crown to begin the battle. We hide in a thicket at the edge of the heath. I go over the plan again and again. My part is to lure the Monster. The sky is overcast, so I can't tell the time with tree shadows as Papa Herne taught me.

After a while, I climb up and perch in the branches of an oak, leaving Half Crown hidden behind the trunk below. I count the forest animals and birds fleeing the Monster's destruction as I remember the countless matches that have passed through my fingers.

As soon as I see Papa Herne's signal – a pair of rooks wheeling overhead – I climb down through the branches onto Half Crown's back.

We race out of the thicket and go looking for the Monster. It doesn't take long to find it. I can hear it coming – a mechanical death, trampling all in its path.

I stop right in front of it, a hundred yards away. I can't see the driver behind the windscreen, but they must see me. The Monster responds angrily: engine roaring, whistle making an ear-splitting screech, dirty fumes flaring from the smokestack.

Then it stamps forward.

"Come on," I say through gritted teeth, "come on."

Old Ma Bogey must have told them who I am, to look out for the boy with the tree-stag.

As the Monster lumbers towards us, Half Crown and I turn on the spot. We gallop ahead, then swerve south in the direction I need the Monster to go.

But when I look back, the stomper has stopped in its tracks. I wonder if there's something wrong. Maybe it needs more coal.

Half Crown and I lope towards the Monster, closer than before. It's only when we're six feet away that it takes another lumbering step.

I realize now what the driver is doing – they want a better chance at catching me. For a heart-wrenching moment, I imagine it's Old Ma Bogey. But as we pull alongside the cabin, the driver leans out from the open side window and I see who it is.

Padlock.

I'm surprised, scared and relieved at the same time. Padlock always loved it when orphans got punished. Nothing would make him happier than catching me and bringing me to Old Ma Bogey.

Padlock scowls then smiles as if he's been thinking the same thing.

This is great.

"Come on, Half Crown," I whisper. "Let's go."

We lead the way and swerve onto the path we need to take.

The Monster comes after us – slow, lumbering, trailing like an out-of-step shadow.

It's working.

Half Crown and I easily stay just ahead. But then the Monster's iron pincer-claw lashes out, trying to grab me. I duck and it misses me by inches. I steer Half Crown away and glance round in horror. This time the Monster's tree-cutting blade reaches out on a long iron arm...

Facing forwards, I aim Half Crown between two Scots pines growing next to each other.

A moment later, the Monster's blade slices through the trunks. The trees tip towards us—

I push Half Crown faster—

We're not fast enough—

The two trunks crash to the ground either side of us, trapping us in a corridor that ends in a bristly mess of pine branches. I brace myself as we hurtle towards the dead end. The scaly trunks are so close that Half Crown nearly grazes against them…but at the last second, with a huge bound, he springs up and leaps over one of them.

Relief rushes through me as we race free and the Monster tramples the fallen pines.

I lean close to Half Crown's ear and press my hand against his bark side. "You did it!"

Once we've put a good distance between us and the Monster, we wait for it to catch up. Then we duck and weave just out of its reach.

We move forward like this – getting too close, escaping away – edging closer and closer to the trap the Hobs have prepared.

When Padlock tries to pincer us between claw and cutting blade, I pull on Half Crown's bark mane and we drop back. The cutting blade misses us and shears off the Monster's claw instead.

The Monster stops and sighs, hissing as steam blasts from its valves.

I circle back, ready to taunt Padlock again. But something is happening with the underside of the Monster. Hatches open. Its load of tree trunks drops to the ground. Then four spoked iron wheels descend.

"This can't be good," I whisper.

I don't wait to find out. I squeeze Half Crown's sides with my legs. "Go! Go!"

As we gallop away, the Monster comes after us, faster now. The distance between us shrinks alarmingly. A moment later, the snarl-painted nose of the Monster bumps against Half Crown's hindquarters. It's as if the painted teeth are trying to eat us.

I crouch forward, clutch on tighter. "Half Crown, can you go any faster?"

Half Crown puts on a fresh burst of speed.

The Monster matches it, engine roaring louder, bumping us again.

I jolt as the whistle shrieks and hunch my shoulders. I'm scared we might fall under the crushing wheels. As I glance back at the front of the Monster, I realize I could climb it, clamber over the steam dome to the driver's cabin.

No, focus on the plan.

I grit my teeth, turn and read the forest ahead. Hazel. Oak. Pine. Elder. Almost there.

A minute later, there's the marker, a deadwood tree. Beyond it is a wide space, a vast clearing edged with grey rock. It's covered in leaves – lots of leaves.

As we bear down on the deadwood tree, I swerve Half Crown out of the Monster's path, then pull up alongside its spinning wheels. I draw to a halt as the Monster speeds into the clearing.

For a split second, I wonder if it really is the right place. But then the front of the Monster lurches forward and drops through the leaf-covered surface.

There's an explosion of water and leaves.

I smile as the Monster hits the water, hissing with fury as its firebox floods.

But then my smile falls away in horror.

The water is deeper than I thought.

Much deeper.

The tail end of the Monster disappears into the dark water. Thick clouds of steam rush up.

The three Hobs appear from their hiding places and join me at the rim of the lake. We watch in silence as wobbling bubbles break the surface…then they're gone. And the only trace of the Monster is the great hole in the leaf-cover.

A long minute drags out. "He's not coming up," I say.

"Who?" says Nissa.

"Padlock – one of the other orphans. He's inside the

Monster." I jump off Half Crown. "He's going to drown unless one of us does something. I'm going in."

Papa Herne is wide-eyed. "Can you swim?"

I don't know, but I have a feeling I can do this. Maybe I'm still charged with the excitement of beating the Monster. I shrug off my cloak, pull off my sweater and jump into the water. It's numbingly cold, but no worse than the water we had to wash in at Harklights. I take several deep breaths and put my head underwater. I can hardly see anything as I dive down into the murky depths. Grey Lake is a twilight world, the hole in the leaf-cover its moon.

A memory flickers inside me.

An old-new memory.

I can swim.

I've been underwater before, but it was brighter... *Diving down to a riverbed where stones are netted with a wavering light. My fingers close round a shining gold circle, a bracelet that someone lost. I'm full of happiness that I found it.* I have the vague feeling that the person who lost the bracelet was someone important to me, but I don't remember who.

As I swim deeper and deeper, the memory fades.

Walls of cold water press in on all sides and there's a tightness in my chest. Beneath me, the Timber Goliath balances on a rock ledge over an underwater abyss.

I kick my legs, propelling myself close to the driver's cabin. Behind the windscreen, Padlock floats in the water over the controls. He's unconscious. I tug the cabin door open and grab Padlock by his collar. Then I drag him through the door.

I kick away as fast as I can.

My lungs ache as I swim upwards. They feel like they're on fire.

When we break the surface, Papa Herne, Nox and Nissa are calling, but I don't hear their words. All I can do is breathe. There's a nasty gash and a bruised imprint of the control levers on Padlock's forehead.

"He's hurt," I say to the Hobs.

I drag him from the water out onto the small beach. Wet leaves stick to us. I thump him between the shoulder blades. He splutters and coughs up water. Breathing again, he collapses onto his back. Then his eyes open, but he says nothing.

"What are we gonna do with him?" says Nissa.

"He's got a head injury," says Papa Herne. "He should

232

stay here. We'll get something to treat it. Wick, you stay with him."

"Quick, let's go," says Papa Herne to the others. "I need help gathering St John's wort, dried petals and leaves."

The trio of bird-riders fly away.

I glance at Padlock, dressed in blue overalls and boots.

Grey Lake is silent. There are no birds in the sky. No deer. It's just me and him. Two orphans from Harklights.

I wait for the flicker of more memories, like the one that bubbled up when I started swimming, but it seems that's all there is right now. All these years I'd thought I'd always been at Harklights, but I was wrong. There was a time before. Another life. I want to dive back down into the depths to see if I can remember anything else.

"You," growls Padlock. "What the *blazes* were you riding?"

I glance over to where Half Crown stands, waiting.

Padlock sits up and clutches his chest, his face twisted as if he's in pain.

"You alright?" I say.

"It's me ticker. I need me pills. Ever since the shotgun kicked me in the chest—"

"What happened? How's Petal?" I cut in.

"About as happy as the rest of 'em. Miss Boggett didn't just punish your friend, she punished all the packsmiths."

A wave of guilt floods through me.

"She makes 'em work faster, longer hours." There's satisfaction in Padlock's voice. "And 'cos of that, she needed to cut down trees quicker. She's already taken down Sixways Wood and most of Waywood Forest. Now she's cutting down Havenwood—"

"How many tree-cutters are there?"

"There's three – were three…"

For a moment, I feel as if I'm falling. That's two left. Two too many.

"Miss Boggett said I needed to learn to shoot. Stags were attacking the Timber Goliaths. I tried her shotgun but then this happened…" He winces and clutches his chest as if his heart is trying to escape. "I got a pistol instead and—"

"*You* shot the stag!" I cut in. There are sharp edges to my words. I fish out the bullet casing from my pocket and thrust it at him. "This is yours then."

Padlock takes it from me with his thick fingers. "Where d'you get it?"

"It doesn't belong in the forest. There'll be no shooting. Not now. Not anytime."

"The forest belongs to Miss Boggett. It's matchwood, all of it." Padlock flinches as he touches the bruise on his head, then coughs. "I need my pills. I'm not going to make it."

Part of me thinks he's faking it. "Don't worry. The others have gone to get you something." Questions press in on all sides, about Old Ma Bogey, about the tree-felling, the shot stag. I feel like I'm underwater again. Suspended. Disorientated. "You'll be okay," I say, trying to reassure him.

Padlock coughs and clutches his chest tighter. "Tell the undertaker to put that on me gravestone. You'll have to get me pillbox from the lake. It's in me jacket."

"Your jacket is gone," I say firmly.

Padlock coughs again – a long dry cough that folds him in half. This time it sounds terrible. Now I'm worried.

When he stops, a vein stands out in his neck and his face is even more twisted in pain.

I think I might be wrong about him faking it.

I wonder how long the Hobs are going to be. St John's wort might take a headache away, but Padlock needs more than that.

"Hawthorn leaves are good for your heart. Wait here, I'll be back."

"I'm not going anywhere," he says.

Half Crown and I race off into the forest. It doesn't take long for us to find a hawthorn. The tree – short, stocky, growing at an angle – is easy to find. As I pick fresh green leaves, I realize I forgot to ask Padlock about Bottletop at Harklights. I hope he's alright too.

When we return to the lake, Padlock is gone. All that's left is the wet shape of him, a dark stain spreading into the stones.

CHAPTER SIXTEEN

MAKING PLANS

Waiting for Papa Herne to return is like the anxious wait for Quota Inspection. Will he be angry when he finds out Padlock has escaped? Will he think I let him go because he was another human? Because I knew him? I'd searched about for footprints but there weren't any. He'd left no tracks. I don't even know how he disappeared so fast.

Thankfully I don't have to wait long. But this time, there's only one bird-rider.

It's Nox.

Great. He's the last Hob I want to tell that I let Padlock get away.

"Where's Papa Herne?" I ask after Nox's blackbird lands on the wet rocks next to me. The blackbird drops a small package wrapped in fabric.

"He's telling the others the truth about the Monster, and how you defeated it. I got honey for the bruising. Where's the human gone?"

I swallow. "He got away."

"Where did he go?" says Nox.

"I don't know. He said he had a bad heart. I went and got some hawthorn. He tricked me."

I wait for Nox to get angry, but his voice has a different tone than I'm used to. It's more gentle, earthy, like Papa Herne's. "It's not yer fault," he says. "Man tricks. It's in his nature. I once got tricked by a human. It were many moons ago – stepped in a butterfly net. If it hadn't been for Papa Herne, I wouldn't have escaped."

My mind whirrs with thoughts. All of them take me to Harklights.

"What's wrong? You defeated the Monster an' stopped Nissa getting hurt."

"I might have stopped the Monster, but there's more."

"More?"

I nod. "Padlock told me there's another two. And if he gets back and tells Old Ma Bogey he's seen me riding a tree-stag, she's going to try and find us. Knowing Old Ma Bogey, she'll send more machines to destroy the forest. I thought trapping the Monster would solve everything, but now I've made things worse. I failed the first rule of Forest Law." I bow my head and turn away. "I'm not good enough to be a Forest Keeper."

"What are you talking about?" cries Nox, startling his blackbird. "Without you, that machine in the lake would still be out there, tearing down trees, killing animals!" He smooths down the bird's ruffled feathers. "Yer brave an' have a good heart. My sons would have been lucky to know you."

"Really?" I feel a pull on my heart.

"Yeah." Nox sniffs.

"I need to go back to Harklights," I say. "I've got to stop her."

"Well, yer not going on yer own. Yer one of us. If you go, then I'm coming with you an' I'll bet the sun an' moon that Papa Herne will too." Nox picks up his reins. "I take it yer thought of a plan."

"Not yet," I say, "but it'll take more than leaves this time."

"Well done, Wick!"

"Defeated the Monster!"

"I always knew you'd be great!" cries the crowd of Hobs when Nox and I enter the clearing. This is followed by cheering and clapping. I didn't think the Hobs could make so much noise.

As I climb down from Half Crown, Mama Herne asks, "What happened to Purlock?"

"Padlock. I – I lost him." I explain what happened.

The crowd erupts into raised voices.

Papa Herne tries shouting, but no one can hear him until Mama Herne bangs pots together.

Clonk. Clonk. Clonk.

Oakhome falls silent.

"Everyone, stay where you are," says Papa Herne with strength in his voice. "We'll stop this once an' for all. We're gonna face this together."

I feel the crowd look at me expectantly, as if I've got all the answers.

"When are we going?" demands Nissa. She stands taller and there's a fierce blaze in her eyes. I guess her fight is back. She juts her chin and tightens her fists. "I might be small, but small things can make a difference." She sounds like Papa Herne, except her tone is more defiant.

I think of all the small things the Hobs have done for me, how much they have added up. Kindness, gentleness, encouragement, love. Showing me what a family can be. They're helping me get better, be braver, stronger.

Papa Herne's eyes shine with pride at Nissa's words.

Mama Herne crosses her arms. "Oh no. You can't go."

"She has to," says Papa Herne evenly. "You should have seen her. She can fly a blackbird better than most."

I clear my throat. "I know she's not a Forest Keeper yet, but she wants to do something to protect the forest."

A smile spreads across Nissa's face.

"We can't lose the forest," says Papa Herne, pulling Mama Herne close as he looks up at me. "If I'd told everyone about the Monster before, we might have been able to work together to stop it. Wick needs all the help he can get now."

Mama Herne nods gravely. "You best be careful," she tells Nissa.

Papa Herne adjusts his hat. "I'll keep an eye on her."

"I will too," I add.

Papa Herne calls down to Genna. "I'll need you to prepare to evacuate Oakhome if the other monsters come. If they do, fly south to Bilberry Hill. You'll be safe in the caves there. The monsters won't be able to get in."

Genna nods. She looks pale and she gazes off into the distance. It's as if she can only see the past, taken back to a place she never wanted to return to.

"What about all our things?" says Finn.

"I'll leave a tree-stag," replies Papa Herne. "Load it up – but only with essentials, mind. Lives are more important than things."

"So, this is the plan," I say, tapping the crude diagram I've made on a cleared patch of forest floor. Lines of twigs mark out everything in Harklights: the yard, the crane, all the rooms, the Bottomless Well. I pick up an acorn and move it. "I'll jump over the yard wall on the back of Half Crown and sneak in through one of the Machine Room windows. Old Ma Bogey keeps some of them open in the day."

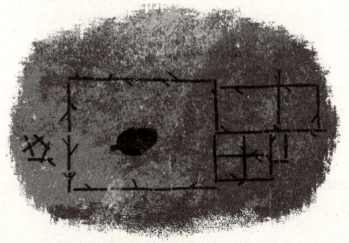

"An' what will we do?" says Nissa, adjusting her catapult.

"You'll be the distraction," I reply. I tap on an old oak leaf. "Once I'm inside, I'll find a way to smash the Machine. I'll use her beating stick if I have to. It's the only way to save the forest. A small destruction to stop a bigger destruction. She won't be able to make any more matches and so there'll be no need to cut down any more trees."

"Wick's right," says Nox and folds his arms.

Papa Herne glances at us both. "I don't like it, but if Wick says it's the only way..."

The words hang in the air.

Nissa clears her throat. "Wick – you said before that she likes to take things away from people. Isn't she still gonna come after us with the other monsters? Even if we stop her Machine?"

I sigh. "Let's hope not."

I change out of my damp sweater and shirt. I put on one of the shirts from the treehouse and fold back the sleeves. Then I put on my cloak.

It takes less than five minutes for us all to get ready. Papa Herne, Nissa and Nox climb onto their bird saddles and take up their reins.

"Okay, let's go." A swirl of fear and hope churns inside me as I climb onto Half Crown's back. Fear at seeing Old Ma Bogey again, hope of rescuing Petal and the others.

There's a snap of black-and-brown wings, then the bird-riders are in the air, flying through the trees.

This is my plan. Everything hinges on this. If it all goes wrong, then it's my fault. It's not only Nissa that could get caught this time, but Papa Herne and Nox too. I push the thoughts away.

I know I can do this. It's what all my time in the forest has been leading to. It's time to stop Old Ma Bogey.

CHAPTER SEVENTEEN

RETURN TO HARKLIGHTS

I gallop along Rabbit Path, the same path we took from Harklights, thinking about how much I've changed. I know what it is to be loved by a family. And I carry the forest within me – the courage of deer, the determination of squirrel, the calm stealth of fox.

"Wick, look!" cries Papa Herne as we stop at the forest edge.

He points to the meadow. It's a blaze of wild colour – lesser celandine, wild daffodil, sweet violet, purple heather. Beyond is Harklights. It's grown. The yard wall to keep the orphans in is higher now. It must be another ten feet tall or more. And rising above it is the crane with the crow-claw.

"Blast it," I mutter. My heart drops. "Half Crown will never be able to jump over that."

Old Ma Bogey must have built it higher after I'd left. I guess she didn't want any more orphans leaping over the wall on the backs of magical tree-stags. And if the wall has changed, what else has?

Papa Herne and the others watch me.

"This doesn't change anything," I say. "I can climb it." I straighten my back and feel warmth stir in my chest.

We cross the meadow. As we approach, the wall looms like a grey-black cliff. As I bring Half Crown to a halt, I notice Scratch sitting in the shadow of the wall. He scampers off as I jump down, then stops ten feet away. He watches with interest as Papa Herne, Nissa and Nox land their birds on the tree-stag's antlers.

"Watch out for Scratch," I say to the Hobs.

The Hobs watch the enormous cat warily as he crouches low to the ground, pretending he's not been seen. His tail swishes slowly from side to side.

I peer up at the wall, remembering the trees I have conquered. "I'm ready for this."

My heart flutters. I'll need to go carefully. This time, there isn't any ivy.

If I slip…

I cut off the thought before it can take hold.

"Shall we fly up?" asks Nox.

"Wait till I get to the top. Wait for my signal." I clear my throat. "Then you make the distraction if you see Old Ma Bogey. But be careful, she's got a shotgun."

Papa Herne nods. "Understood."

I breathe out deeply. "Okay. Good luck to us all."

I say goodbye to Half Crown, then start to make my way up the wall, still trying not to think about there being no ivy. Instead I think of myself as ivy, clinging on.

The spaces between the bricks make perfect hand- and footholds. About halfway up, my old fear grips me, rooting me to the spot, but I wrench myself free. I won't let it hold me back.

When I reach the top, I peer over and down into the yard. A rush of Harklights memories comes flooding back: bowls of porridge, Old Ma Bogey's beating stick, her iron thumb pinching my ear. For a moment, I feel a sort of hollowness in the pit of my stomach. Like the opposite of homesickness.

Everything is mostly as it was before. The Bottomless Well sits in one corner. The crane claw stands nearby. The yard is even emptier without the gnarled old tree. But Harklights is quiet, which is strange as it's not a Sunday. The Machine isn't running. The chimney isn't belching yellow smoke.

I swing a leg over the wall and signal to Papa Herne. My heart thuds in my chest as I try to find a foothold on the other side.

The porch door opens and the orphans file out mechanically, without feeling.

My heart rises as I see them, but it twists with guilt knowing they've been punished. They look so tired.

Old Ma Bogey appears behind them. Her hair is still scraped into a bun, but she's wearing a new fitted coat and long skirt, both emerald green.

"Look – who – is – back!" she cries out, emphasizing

each word. "Have you come to rescue the others or did you miss the meals?"

I don't answer.

"Padlock told me you were asking questions. I *knew* you were coming."

The orphans look up. Some don't look happy to see me. Others stare in wonder, and I think back to the moment they last saw me, leaping over the wall on a tree-stag. Petal appears alongside Old Ma Bogey.

Relief rushes through me. "Petal, you're alright—" My voice breaks.

"Wick!" cries Petal. She looks more shocked than pleased to see me.

Old Ma Bogey knocks Petal aside. "Let us give Wick a welcome!" she snarls as she raises her pistol. "If anyone helps him, there will be *more* punishments."

She aims and fires. Gunshots punch the air.

Bang.

Bang.

Ricochet sparks spray from the brickwork beneath my feet. Instinctively I duck.

The bird-riding Hobs swoop down over the yard. The blackbirds' wings are outstretched, their long feathers like fingers. I can't help but think that together we carry all the hope of the forest.

As Old Ma Bogey watches the blackbirds swerve away from the crane, I silently thank the Hobs for their distraction. I catch Petal's eye and point to the small cabin housing the crane controls.

Petal nods. She slips away from Old Ma Bogey and dashes over to the cabin, ducking inside. She pulls on the levers and moves the crane arm. It stutters with stop-starts, then swings round towards me on the wall. When the claw is near enough, I take a deep breath, reach out and grab hold of the chain. Then I'm circling over the yard – a moving target standing on top of the claw. Old Ma Bogey and the orphans sweep past beneath me.

My old fear grips me again. I'm a breath away from falling.

There's a crunching sound. The crane stops, then starts up again.

Papa Herne, Nox and Nissa circle in the air astride their blackbirds.

Old Ma Bogey takes aim.

Bang.

Bang.

Bang.

There's an explosion of feathers and all three blackbirds drop from the sky like overripe fruit.

My blood turns cold. "PAPA HERNE! NOX! NISSA!"

The Hobs tumble through the air. I'm plunged into a world of horror. This isn't happening. How can everything go wrong so fast?

Old Ma Bogey shouts to the orphans. "Catch the little people! I want them alive!"

Why alive?

Petal is still in the crane cabin, but the rest of the orphans race wildly to catch the Hobs.

Fear clenches my heart. "No!"

Old Ma Bogey reloads her pistol and lines me up in her sights.

I hold onto the chain tightly and wait for the death-strike. My heart pounds wildly – it's not ready to give up on life just yet.

I look down.

The crane arm spins me in a wide arc, across the yard and towards the main building…

As I near a low section of the factory roof, I see the iron walkway across the back wall of the Machine Room. Then I spot large twin trapdoors. This must be where the trees are dropped in. It's madness to jump.

I look back down to the yard and see Nissa. One of the orphans is holding her, but it doesn't stop her pulling her catapult back to her ear, aiming a stone at Old Ma Bogey, who's still pointing her gun at me.

As Old Ma Bogey squeezes the trigger, she jolts.

Bang.

There's a sting in my shoulder. Blood blooms on my cloak.

I lose my grip on the chain—

And fall—

It's about a ten foot drop through the air—

The closed trapdoors break my fall temporarily, before they slam open and I drop down again into half-darkness. A searing pain shoots through my ankle as I land in what could be a giant's thimble. I stifle a cry. I won't give Old Ma Bogey the satisfaction of knowing I'm hurt. I unbutton the top of my shirt and see that the shot didn't go through my shoulder. It's just a graze. The bleeding isn't too bad.

Nissa saved me. She was right. Small things can make a difference.

I take a corner of my cloak and press it down on the graze, then peer around at the high metal walls that rise up on all sides. There's no escape door or ladder. Only scars and dents, where trees have scraped and knocked. And there's a smell of resin.

A whirring noise starts up. The Machine is waking up from its sleep. The floor beneath me gives way. I'm funnelled into a narrow chute, then fall onto a conveyor belt with high sloped sides. When I was a packsmith, I never really thought about where matches came from. But this is where trees come to be made into Everstrikes.

Panic hits me. My heart thuds even wilder – a bird in a bone-cage trying to get free. With shaking fingers, I try to get to my feet, but jagged pain crumples me. My ankle won't take my weight.

A circular blade carves through the middle of the conveyor. I roll out of the way but I'm not quick enough. Part of my Forest Keeper cloak is cut away. A shudder runs through me as I feel the heat of the spinning blade at my back.

Then another chute drops me down into the next section. I lie rigid – wincing and terrified – as an arc of ferocious blades fall into place all around me, making a tunnel of death. The blades pass by, inches away, shaving off imaginary bark. I sit up, needing to see what's next, to see what deadly pieces the Machine will put into play and how – *or if* – I can avoid them. I press myself flat just in time, clenching my teeth as more blades come slicing sideways out of the wall.

Ahead in the darkness, there's a thunderous sound. I can't see anything but I know what's coming. Here must be where the wood is cut into smaller and smaller pieces. I won't be able to dodge the blades much longer. I reach up, fumbling for the high side of the conveyor, but it is unexpectedly low. Agony screams in my ankle as I haul myself up the side, heave myself over.

I collapse onto the deck plate, and take staggering breaths, relieved to be away from the blades. Then it dawns on me how double lucky I am. Not only am I still alive, but I'm *inside* the Machine Room. Now I just need to find the controls.

I force myself up and limp my way along a dark passageway that weaves around and through the Machine. I'm in the belly of a giant beast – the metal beams overhead are the bones of its ribcage. Steam hisses as it rises from the floor. It feels as if the Machine is breathing. Somewhere nearby, the thunder and thrum of cutting blades is replaced with a threshing sound. I stop a moment and rest against one of the metal panels. It's warm and humming, almost alive.

At the end of the passage, I step out into light and turn a corner. There, by the cauldron, is the furnace with huge snaking pipes. There's something else – the control panel. And by its side is an open toolbox.

I limp over and heave up a long spanner.

As I'm about to strike down on the dials and valves that run everything, there's a blast of steam from a vent. Then a hand with an unmistakable metal thumb reaches through the wall of vapour and grabs hold of me.

I recoil in terror, but my wrist is locked in an iron grip.

"OH NO YOU DON'T!" barks Old Ma Bogey over the hiss of steam.

CHAPTER EIGHTEEN

THE CROSSBOW

I crumple as Old Ma Bogey squeezes my wrist in her crushing grip. I drop the spanner onto the deck plate. *Clang.*

"So, you came back to smash my Machine!" She's breathing heavily and her eyes are filled with fury. There's a cut on her cheek, where the stone from Nissa's catapult must have struck. I wonder if Padlock had the guts to tell her about the Timber Goliath in the lake.

Someone else moves in the shadows: eyes wide, skin pale as paper. I can hardly believe my eyes.

Bottletop is dressed in mechanic's overalls and a cap.

He isn't trembling. Instead of a matchbox, he's holding an oil rag.

"Get back to work!" barks Old Ma Bogey. "Check the valves!"

Bottletop flinches.

I wonder how many times she's beaten him since I left.

I lift my twisted ankle as Old Ma Bogey drags me past the furnace at a brisk pace. She's very strong. It's as if she's a human machine that runs on anger.

"Where are you taking me?" I try and wrestle free from her grip, but she squeezes tighter.

"To see your *little* friends," she growls.

I know Nissa was caught when she fell, but what about Papa Herne? And what about Nox? I picture Scratch licking his whiskers.

My insides tense. Even if they're alright, we'll never be able to escape. How could I have brought them here?

We pass something odd – a brass telescope, its sight-end pressed against the wall.

I stare at Old Ma Bogey.

"Spyhole. I've got them all over Harklights. I see everything."

"The matchbox models," I breathe. "*You* saw me making them..."

Old Ma Bogey nods. "I wanted to see how far you would go. You are quite a maker. Reminds me of how I was as a girl. Making steam-powered toys. Clever engines that walked."

"But you told me one of the orphans snitched on me. You tried to tell me it was Petal!"

As I turn, the jagged pain flares in my ankle. I take a sharp breath, but Old Ma Bogey continues to drag me down a flight of metal stairs to the ground floor. I know where we are. These are the stairs I passed every day going to the Match Room. She wrenches open the green door and we step into the corridor that runs past the dining room and Old Ma Bogey's office. We turn into the hall with the grandfather clock, then into Old Ma Bogey's drawing room. The high-backed armchair is still by the fireplace. But now there are more weapons hung on the wall.

Petal is shut in the cabinet with wire-mesh panels. Next to it is a birdcage.

"You shouldn't have come back," says Petal.

"I had to," I reply. "I wanted us to escape together—"

"Wick!"

"We thought you were dead!" It's Nissa and Nox, crying out through the cage bars.

"I'm alright. Where's Papa Herne?"

262

"Somewhere safe," says Old Ma Bogey, her mouth twisting.

I try and pull myself free from her grip but it only makes my wrist burn. "Let Petal and the Hobs go. It's me you want. I was the one who ran away... I'll stay this time. I'll be a packsmith again."

Old Ma Bogey laughs. It's a scary high ringing sound. She tilts her head right back and I can see the upside-down horseshoe curve of her teeth.

I've never heard her laugh in all the years I can remember.

"Who said *anything* about you packing more matches? I've got other orphans who are faster packers than you."

She studies me, her sharp eyes skewering me like pins. "Father told me that machines are nothing but cogs and wheels. Operators are their hearts, and you are going to be the heart of the Machine. You are going to be responsible for chopping up every tree in Havenwood Forest. Then all your cut-to-pieces trees will be boxed and shipped across Empire Britannica!"

I picture the matchboxes as cardboard coffins and feel the strength go out of my legs. All the hope goes out of me too. "No…no."

"And if you don't, I'm going to let Scratch play with your little friends. And we all know how that ends."

Nox, Nissa and Petal are horror-struck.

Old Ma Bogey leans forward, her eyes searching mine, then she smiles as if a light in my eyes has died.

At this moment, Bottletop hovers in the doorway.

"Why aren't you with the Machine?" barks Old Ma Bogey.

Bottletop flinches again. "I came to tell you something," he whispers. "Miss Boggett, I…er…" Then from somewhere his voice suddenly gathers strength and he stands straight-backed. "I tipped over the cauldron. I reckon we've got a minute before the Machine explodes."

"WHAT?" roars Old Ma Bogey.

She lets go of me. I duck away from her as she grabs a shotgun from the wall and aims it at Bottletop, her fingers trembling. It's as if her rage is so big she can't even think properly.

Bottletop disappears into the corridor.

I lift the cabinet latch to free Petal, then grab the crossbow off its resting hooks.

Petal climbs out and grabs the birdcage with Nissa and Nox. "Wick! It's time to go!" she says. "We've got to get the other orphans to safety!"

"Petal – stop!" yells Old Ma Bogey. The shotgun wavers.

Petal freezes by the door.

"Let Petal and the Hobs go." I lift the crossbow and aim it at Old Ma Bogey. It's not heavy, but it's loaded and has weight. The weight of ending someone's life.

Old Ma Bogey growls. "You couldn't shoot me."

I don't answer. The tip of the crossbow bolt shakes. I can't keep it still.

She puts down the shotgun. Then she reaches into her pocket and pulls out Papa Herne, dangling him by his Forest Keeper cloak. "Oh, don't worry, he's still alive."

His body hangs limp, his eyes are shut. His magic staff is missing.

There's a madness in her eyes. "But if you want him, you will have to try and stop me!"

I tense up, get a firmer grip on the crossbow. Line her up in my sights. But she's right, I can't do it.

There has to be another way.

She drops Papa Herne back into her pocket and strides through the door, turning towards the factory.

She's going the wrong way. Heading towards the Machine that's about to explode.

Petal and the Hobs give me a worried look.

"Go," I say firmly. "I'll catch up with you."

Petal nods and leaves with the birdcage.

I chase after Old Ma Bogey, ignoring my ankle, which feels like fire. She barrels through the green door and up the metal stairs. When I catch up with her, she's by the tipped-over cauldron. Thick match-tip mixture, like red porridge or lava, creeps towards the furnace. It's too late – there's no way she can stop it.

With a crazed look in her eyes, she runs down the dark corridor that weaves through the Machine.

Where's she going? Is she heading for another exit? Or is she leading me into a trap?

I grit my teeth and limp after her. I hope Petal and the others are somewhere safe.

I'm halfway down a passage when there's a wild roar. A solid wall of force blasts me off my good foot.

This is the dragon.

I curl into a ball as fire and shrapnel whistle past my head.

When I look up, there's a gaping hole that runs through the middle of the Machine and out the end wall of the factory.

The passage is filled with smoke, steam, rubble and dust. The grey silhouette of Old Ma Bogey staggers to her feet and clambers, coughing, through the hole. I can't believe it. We both survived.

I grab the crossbow and get to my feet with ringing ears.

At the end wall, the view through the hole has me reeling.

The iron walkway outside no longer clings to the wall. One end leans out like a gangplank, overhanging the yard. And the Bottomless Well.

The walkway tilts. It's not safe. But Old Ma Bogey is there on it, stepping further and further away. She knows about my nightmares. I know what she's doing. This is punishment – she wants to make me suffer as much as possible.

My old fear of heights sticks to my bones, but it's only for a second.

"Stop!" I yell.

Old Ma Bogey grunts and keeps walking – then she loses her footing and slides along the sloping walkway.

"Papa Herne!" My heart leaps to my mouth.

For a sickening moment, she slides over the edge—

Then – *clang* – her iron-thumbed hand grabs onto the walkway's end.

With my heart kicking wildly, I step onto the walkway. There's a metallic creak as it sways.

I'm not sure it can take our combined weight.

I drop the crossbow. Instead of pushing my fear away, I hold onto it tightly. I realize my fear of the Well was never just about heights, it was about losing others.

I won't lose Papa Herne. He's family.

I soak strength from the Keeper cloak around my shoulders, strength from all the love the Hobs have given me.

Using the handrail for support, I hobble to the end of the walkway.

"Quick – give me your hand," I cry. I never thought I'd ever try and save Old Ma Bogey. But I need to. It's the only way to save Papa Herne.

As I get closer, Old Ma Bogey holds up Papa Herne by his cloak.

"You want *this*?"

"Miss Boggett, don't…"

"Then go and get it!" She throws Papa Herne up in the air—

I'm seized by horror as I raise my arm—

Fingers outstretched—

For a flickering moment, he's out of reach—

Then something deep within takes over, an instinct that will always be part of me.

A machine instinct.

I grab Papa Herne. The same way I grab a handful of matches.

I sink to the walkway, cradling him in my hands.

"You took everything from me!" bellows Old Ma Bogey. She grabs at my sleeve, pulls and leans back. "Now, I will take you…from everything!"

I stow Papa Herne in my shirt pocket and hold onto the handrail with both hands. My fingers begin to lose their grip. There's a tearing sound. My sleeve splits at the shoulder. As the split widens, so do Old Ma Bogey's eyes.

I can't help but watch as she falls—

Through the air—

Into the open mouth of the Bottomless Well.

CHAPTER NINETEEN
THE SMOKING CABINET

The orphans are shell-shocked from the explosion. At first they have the same blank faces as the Hobs did when the stag destroyed their nest-huts. But these soon turn into grins and crooked smiles.

The Machine is broken.

Old Ma Bogey is gone.

Padlock and Scratch are nowhere to be seen.

Petal, Bottletop and the others fill me in on how Padlock came back to Harklights to tell Old Ma Bogey that I'd be coming and then left quickly. I tell them about the Timber Goliath, the one that sank, and rescuing Padlock from Grey Lake.

Papa Herne is cradled in my hands. When he comes round, he takes a shuddering breath and we all sigh with relief. Nissa and Nox hug him, sobbing.

My eyes glisten with tears.

When they've finished hugging, I tell Papa Herne about the explosion and Old Ma Bogey and the Well.

"You did good, Wick," he says. "I knew you would."

"I wouldn't have been able to do it without help from my friends. Thanks for saving me, back there in the yard," I say to Nissa. "Old Ma Bogey was going to shoot me."

"I know you'd have done the same for me," she says with bright eyes.

Petal finds the fire buckets. We put out the fires in the Machine Room. The Machine is beyond repair. There's no way it will ever run again.

While Nox, Nissa and the rest of the orphans are in the kitchens, celebrating by breaking into the pantry and gorging themselves on Fry's chocolate and tins of peaches, I head through the ruins to Old Ma Bogey's office. Papa Herne rides in my shirt pocket, Petal and Bottletop walking behind us. It's strange to think that Old Ma Bogey is really gone. I don't think it's really sunk in yet. I keep expecting her to appear with her beating stick or a gun.

"She had files on us," Petal says. "We'll be able to find out who we are."

When we reach the office, Petal lifts a rattling bunch of keys from her pocket and unlocks the door. I push it open.

There's a smell of smoke inside. A wooden filing cabinet stands by the window. The top is grazed with a huge charred mark; a trickle of thin smoke rises from its seams.

We rush over. Just as I'm about to reach for the top drawer, Petal says, "Careful, the handle might be hot."

Bottletop hands me his oil rag. "Here – use this."

I wrench the drawer open. Thick black smoke rolls out. What's left of the files are still burning. I pull out a sheaf of brittle black pages. I can just about make out the faint lettering before they crumble to ash.

Smoke stings my eyes before they crowd with tears.

Papa Herne coughs.

"G-gone," sobs Petal.

Bottletop hugs her.

"Old Ma Bogey must have set fire to them when she heard I was coming back, just in case I got this far," I say, my voice hard-edged.

I wipe my eyes, closing the top drawer and pulling open the bottom one. It's divided into a grid of different sections. In each square sits a small object. Thimble, coin, bottle top. "The things she used to name us." I glance over the scorched remains of fabric swatches and what looks like a lantern wick. "But how are they going to tell us anything?"

Petal and Bottletop give blank stares, then Petal says, "Now we'll never find our parents."

"Why would we go looking for them?" says Bottletop. "They abandoned us."

I nod, close the drawer and swallow the lump in my throat.

Papa Herne looks up at Petal and Bottletop. "You could come an' live with us in the forest. All of the orphans. We got plenty of space... You don't have to give me an answer now, take yer time to think on it."

Petal and Bottletop nod mutely, their eyes pricked with tears.

Guilt rises in me like the smoke from the cabinet. I clear my throat. "Sorry you got caught when we escaped," I say to Petal. "I meant to come back sooner—"

Petal smiles. "I know I said to escape without me, but I'm glad you came back."

She throws her arms around me and hugs me, being

careful of my grazed shoulder. "I've been telling stories about you and your magic stag, going off on adventures."

I hug her back awkwardly, heat rising in my cheeks. "Careful of Papa Herne."

"Yeah, sorry," says Petal, stepping back.

Papa Herne beams up at us from my shirt pocket. "I'm alright. No harm done."

"Come on," I mutter. "There must be something useful we can find in here, something about us."

I put Papa Herne down on the desk, next to Old Ma Bogey's beating stick.

We search the office, pulling open drawers and cupboards. There's a ledger listing the stock of matchboxes, a notebook filled with dozens of sketches for Old Ma Bogey's mechanical beetles and Timber Goliaths, broken pen nibs, a dried bottle of ink. But there are no more orphan records, no tin soldiers, none of our old clothes or any of the other things that were confiscated.

I hesitate. The words to tell Papa Herne about the dead Hob in the bell jar are on my tongue, but I have to get them out. "Remember I told you there was a dead Hob. He's, um, in here." I pick up the bell jar and knock it against the edge of the desk. The glass breaks and falls away like eggshell.

Papa Herne swallows as I set the base of the bell jar down. He unfastens his Forest Keeper cloak, throws it over the dead Hob, then takes off his hat and holds it to his chest. "I don't recognize him, but he's a Hob all the same. We'll take him back to the forest, where he belongs. Give him a proper burial."

Petal picks up the beating stick and brandishes it as if it's a sword.

"Well that's going down the Well," I say without thinking.

She frowns. "Why?"

"Because of all the beatings."

Petal examines the stick. "It's not the stick's fault. I don't think it wanted to hit anyone. Maybe it could become something new – the Story Stick."

"I don't know. I still think we should get rid of it." I reach out a hand. "Can I have it?"

Petal is about to hand the stick over, then she pulls back and grins. "You're going to throw it – I know it!"

"No, I'm not." I match her grin. I can't hide anything from Petal. "Okay, I am."

"Wick, Petal!" cries Bottletop just then. "You should come and look at this!"

We rush over to where he stands by a glass display cabinet. I say nothing, daring to hope he might have found something with our real names on.

The glass of the cabinet is covered in thick dust, but Bottletop has wiped a patch clean.

I catch a glimpse of tiny winged figures pinned like

butterflies. I've seen figures like them before. At the Wandwood Tree. Different, but the same.

Papa Herne calls over from the desk. "What is it?"

"Wood sprites," I say.

Papa Herne crosses to the edge of the desk. "I want to see them."

Bottletop turns the brass catch and lifts the glass lid.

I bring Papa Herne over to the cabinet. He jumps off my hand and lands on the velveteen cushion. He leans forward, examining the row of five pale green figures with their outstretched dragonfly wings. Next to them is a row of three pairs of human-sized spectacles with hexagonal green lenses. The lenses are just like the one at the Wandwood Tree, the one that made the invisible wood sprites visible. I have the vague feeling I've seen the spectacles somewhere before, but the memory fizzles like a wet match.

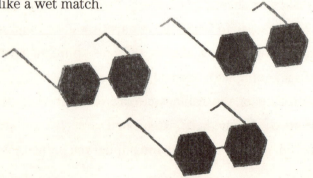

Petal and Bottletop are spellbound by the pinned winged things.

I'm dazed too. How can we see them without the lenses?

"They can't be dead," Papa Herne's voice rises in disbelief. "Wood sprites are spirit. They never die. They must be in a deep sleep. Hibernating." He pulls the pins out of them. Then he shakes one gently, trying to wake them, but they don't move. "You can't be dead."

A bolt of cold runs through me.

Papa Herne's face is full of sorrow as he climbs onto my hand. Bottletop goes to close the glass lid, but Petal stops him. She's still clutching the beating stick. We stand with our heads bowed for a minute or so, then Bottletop, me and Papa Herne slowly head for the door, but Petal stays by the cabinet.

"Wait!" Petal cries out suddenly. "They're breathing!"

There's a papery sigh as we turn back. The sprite opens their eyes.

"They're still alive," gasps Bottletop.

"What...happened?" the sprite says in a rasping voice.

"Someone pinned..." I clear my throat and start again. "Someone caught you and pinned you."

The sprite closes their eyes again and their tiny brow furrows. "Boggett," they say, their voice barely above a whisper. "He was a friend...of nature...but he hurt us."

The other sprites slowly awaken too.

"What's happening to them?" says Petal, touching my elbow. "They're turning see-through."

Papa Herne grins. "They're getting better."

I pick up a pair of the spectacles and try them on. The sprites are solid again. I tap one of the lenses. "These let you see them." I pick up the other pairs and hand them to Petal and Bottletop.

"These are just like the spectacles the man's wearing—" says Petal.

"What man?" I cut in.

Petal pushes the spectacles up to the bridge of her nose. "You know, the one in the photograph on the main stairs. The one we think is Old Ma Bogey's father."

A memory of the photograph burns brightly in my mind. "You're right." I lean close to the sprites. "Did Boggett build a treehouse in the forest?"

The sprites clutch their throats.

"Shall I go get some water?" says Bottletop.

"Good idea," replies Papa Herne.

Bottletop returns with a glass tumbler and sets it down on the side table.

"Thank you," chorus the sprites as they dive into the water without disturbing the surface.

We watch them in awe as they linger in the water. They don't look as if they are drinking, they just stay still.

Then the sprites pass through the glass and back into the air. A healthy apple-green colour returns to them – their faces look less drawn, their eyes brighter. I know they must be getting better because they become as talkative as the ones at the Wandwood Tree. High, silvery voices. Words that run into each other. "Boggett and his daughter – do not matter any more – they're gone—"

It feels good to hear this. But I still have questions about who Old Ma Bogey's father was and what he did.

"How is the orchard – and garden – our beautiful garden—"

"Gone," says Papa Herne.

The sprites look at each other, confused. "But it is not winter – the garden should be filled – with flowers—" They loop in the air, diving, rising, one trailing another, until I can't tell who leads and who follows. They seem upset at the loss. Then they chatter, bright with the memories of how beautiful the garden must have been. "The orchard – and the garden – we can bring them back—"

"Where're you going?" I say, as the sprites break their loop and fly across Old Ma Bogey's office.

"To find our friends – we have been asleep – for far too long—"

Papa Herne's face shines as his smile grows. "They'll be back."

I smile too, remembering the tree by the sunlit fox that was covering an old wound with new bark. Nature has ways to repair itself.

CHAPTER TWENTY
UNEXPECTED GUESTS

As Petal cleans and bandages my grazed shoulder, Nissa and Papa Herne sit with me on a small stack of Everstrikes matchboxes.

"Papa," says Nissa, "did you mean what you said about training me to be a Forest Keeper?"

Papa Herne nods.

"Then I do want to train. It's everything I've ever wanted."

His shining eyes and wide smile tell me he couldn't be happier.

After a while, a flock of bird-riders arrive. It's the rest of the Hob tribe. We gather in the canteen, Hobs and orphans,

eating a victory feast. Cold meats from the meat safe. Bread, cheese and honey from the larder. Jam tarts, crumpets, raisin cakes and Fry's chocolate from the pantry. There's everything but porridge. The Hobs sit on handkerchief picnic blankets among the food. They eat bread and cheese off tiny plates from a doll's house Wingnut found in Old Ma Bogey's bedroom, and button plates which Tiggs wants as treasure.

I sit with Bottletop and Petal on one of the benches. Across from us are Papa Herne, Mama Herne and Nissa. Wingnut draws chalk pictures with Nox and a group of orphans coo over Baby Tiya. Further down the table, another group play with Linden and Tiggs.

I try honey for the first time. It's thick and sweet and tastes of the scent of flowers. I don't think I've eaten anything that tasted better.

"Liquid gold," says Papa Herne.

I have a warm feeling from sharing the Hobs with everyone and not having to hide parts of me.

"Thanks for helping us stop Old Ma Bogey," I say to Bottletop.

He smiles. "Don't worry about it."

"How'd you get out of packing matchboxes?"

"Padlock."

"Padlock?"

"He told Old Ma Bogey that a broken machine part couldn't be fixed. I told her he was wrong."

"You said that?"

Bottletop nods. "I used to fix machines in another factory, before I came here. Old Ma Bogey gave me a chance and I fixed it. After that, she made me work in the Machine Room. I didn't know you were back until I saw you with her. And when she said you were planning on smashing the Machine – well, it got me thinking."

"More than that," I say. "You did something – something amazing."

While we eat, Petal goes outside to get some fresh air. It's not long before she's back, eyes wide as if she's seen a ghost. "You've got to come and see this! Quick!"

We race through the hall, orphans carrying Hobs.

When we reach the yard, there's a cluster of tree-stags behind the main gates. Half Crown is there at the front of them. The gates squeak their complaint as the tree-stags push against them.

Excited chatter erupts among the orphans. "It's that thing—"

"I thought I was dreaming—"

"Told you it was real," says Petal to the others.

"They want us to them let in," I say.

We race over to the gates with Old Ma Bogey's keys. The key for the gates is the easiest to find. It's the largest one, the colour of a storm cloud.

As soon as the key turns in the lock, the tree-stags push through the gates and stampede into the yard. Somehow, we don't get trampled as they circle round the yard, wooden hooves kicking up dry dust.

"What do they want?" yells Petal.

"I don't know," I murmur.

The tree-stags spread out, each of them stopping in different places. Then Half Crown circles round them and waits by the orphanage.

Green light shimmers in the air around all of the tree-stags except for Half Crown. One by one, they transform: turning and twisting, antlers to branches, back into trees. The orphans stare, stunned into silence.

"Did you do this?" I say to Papa Herne.

"No."

I put on the green spectacles. Tiny winged figures flit through the air around them.

"The wood sprites came back," I say.

Petal and Bottletop look through the other pairs, then pass them around to the rest of the orphans.

Across the grey sky, a low dark cloud speeds towards us. As it gets close, I realize it's a cloud of birds – thousands and thousands of them.

"What's happening?" whispers Bottletop as the yard is plunged into shadow.

"The forest is coming to Harklights," says Papa Herne from my shirt pocket.

A small flock of sparrows fly out of the dark cloud above us and swoop down with wood sprites alongside them. The sparrows scatter leaf-mould and peat moss from their claws, then return to the bird swarm. The sprites stay behind, zigzagging like dragonflies over the ground.

"I don't see how a handful of soil is going to do anything," says one of the orphans.

Papa Herne says nothing.

Almost immediately, another wave of birds swoops down. Buzzards, sparrowhawks, red kites, crows, alongside rooks, doves and countless others. All of them drop a rain of soil and small plants.

Some of the orphans duck, others run back inside for

safety, as if we're under attack. But Petal, Bottletop and I know different.

"They're putting the garden back," whispers Petal, shielding her eyes.

I nod, with a massive grin on my face.

Before long, the yard is carpeted with a thick layer of black soil, and is beginning to look like a garden again. More wood sprites appear, joining the others.

"Why didn't you ask the sprites to help you with the Monster?" I say to Papa Herne.

"They don't fight. They only help things grow."

The gathered sprites hover and hold their hands out, palm down, over the new garden. There's more green light, rising, rushing, shimmering. Grass and moss grow. Trees unfurl their leaves. Clusters of blossom buds burst, their flowers like fireworks. White and pink and pink-white. Petal is right, the cherry blossom trees *do* look like clouds.

Petal claps her hands. "We are going to have so much fruit!"

One of the wood sprites flits towards us with a robin holding Papa Herne's lost staff in its beak.

"You will be needing this," says the wood sprite.

"Thank you." Papa Herne bows his head and takes his staff.

As the cloud of birds leave, the hair on my arms stands up.

Wingnut whistles and says, "That was unexpected."

"You can say that again," says Petal.

There's a break in the grey clouds. Shafts of brilliant sunlight lance down. We explore the new walled garden. The moss and grass is a thick green carpet fringed with ferns, shrubs, bushes and banks of sweet-scented flowers. Nox smiles when I tell the orphans to keep to the grass paths and not to trample any of the plants.

Half Crown gives rides to the orphans and Hobs.

Others climb in the trees or sit under the blossom or watch butterflies.

Wingnut, Petal, Bottletop and me cover the Bottomless Well with planks of scorched wood from the Machine Room. Just before we drag the last plank across, I stand on the edge and look down.

I feel a huge wave of relief wash through me.

Old Ma Bogey has really gone.

It's all over.

No more beatings. No more packing matches.

Petal moves close and stands by my side. "You're right, the beating stick should go."

She throws the stick down the Well.

We watch it in silence—

Spinning through the air—

Shrinking as it falls—

Till it's swallowed by darkness.

Afterwards, we sit with Papa Herne and talk about what we are going to do about the other Timber Goliaths.

"Old Ma Bogey may be gone," I say, "but the drivers don't know that. Not yet. They're still out there, cutting down trees."

"They'll be easy to stop," says Papa Herne. "Now we know they're not monsters."

"How?" I ask.

"Well, if ivy vine can stop a rampaging stag in its tracks, I'm sure it can pull a driver away from the controls of a machine."

"Then what will you do?" asks Petal.

"We'll scare them away with tree-stags or tree-somethings." Papa Herne rubs his chin. "Maybe we could even dream a bit bigger."

As the sun lowers in the sky, the wall's shadow stretches across the garden.

Papa Herne calls to Half Crown. "We'd better be getting back."

"But you can stay in the doll's house," calls out a small voice.

"Thanks," says Papa Herne, "but we got some forest animals that we need to take care of."

"We've...er...been talking," says Petal, "about your offer—"

Papa Herne raises his hand. "You got time enough to decide."

Petal smiles. "We're going to stay here, for now. It's the only place most of us have ever known."

The rest of the orphans nod their heads.

"I wanted to escape with Wick before, but I never wanted to leave the others... We can grow vegetables and fruit for ourselves. The sprites said they'd help us."

"What about adults?" I say.

"We don't need them. Old Ma Bogey didn't exactly look after us," replies Bottletop.

"And if anyone comes asking questions?"

"We'll tell them Miss Boggett is sick in bed," says Petal, "and send them away. Don't worry – we'll be fine. I don't think Padlock will ever come back. He said he was going to London to make his fortune."

"Well, the offer is always there. An' yer welcome to visit us any time," says Papa Herne. "What about you, Wick? Are you staying?"

Petal and Bottletop's longing glances tell me they'd like me to stay. I pinch my lip. Part of me wants to. The orphans were my family for so long.

"No," I say finally, "I want to finish my Forest Keeper training and replant all the lost trees." I glance over to Petal. "But I'll come back and see you all the time. Harklights isn't far."

A smile lurks at the corner of Petal's mouth. "You'd better. We'll keep you a chalked-out space on the floor."

"Thanks. What are you going to do with the Machine?"

"I'll think of something," says Petal, leaning close to Bottletop. "And let me know if you ever need any Everstrikes, I'm sure we could spare you a few boxes."

"I will," I say.

The Hob bird-riders take to the air and circle the garden before flying away over the wall.

I climb up onto the back of Half Crown, running my hand down his rough bark. Nox and Nissa stand in his rack of antlers. There are wax-paper parcels strapped to their backs.

"Chocolate," says Nox before I say anything.

Nissa eyes the crossbow that Wingnut cradles in his arms. "I'm definitely making a bow an' arrow when we get back."

Papa Herne adjusts his hat. "We'll have to see."

Nissa presses her mouth into a thin line. Then she smiles.

As we ride off, I turn round and wave at the orphans crowded around Petal. The garden gathers around them in a green hug. Above the garden, the tall chimney points at the sky. Smokeless.

"They're gonna be alright," says Papa Herne, still smiling.

"I think you're right," I say. Then I look ahead across the wild meadow to the wall of trees.

Home.

THE END

PAPA HERNE'S GLOSSARY
OF FOREST HOMES

Every creature needs somewhere safe to call home. Here are a few habitats that Forest Keepers look after.

Bed: The place on the ground where a deer sleeps. Beds are made of flattened bracken, grass or leaves.

Burrow: A tunnel or hole dug out for habitation. Frogs, foxes, badgers, rabbits, lizards and some birds, such as kingfishers, burrow into the ground.

Den: Foxes make their homes by burrowing underground. Dens have a tunnel with a chamber or chambers for raising their young and storing food. Sometimes foxes live in unused setts or warrens.

Drey: Squirrels make their ball-shaped nests in trees using twigs and leaves. They are lined with soft moss and feathers.

Eyrie: The nest of an eagle, hawk, or other bird of prey. Eyries are perched high up, in tall trees, or on rocky ledges. They are made using branches and sticks, and lined with heather and grasses.

Form: Hare homes are made by flattening grass on the ground.

Hive: Bees make their homes by eating honey and turning it into beeswax, which they produce from their abdomen. Hives consist of sheets of hexagonal cells with evenly set spaces in between for the bees to walk on.

Nest: Birds make cup-shaped structures to shelter their eggs and raise their young. Nests are made using mud and twigs, and lined with moss, feathers, grasses and leaves. Tawny owls like to nest in hollow trees, but sometimes they use crows' nests or dreys.

Roost: Birds, like most bats, rest in the high branches of trees. Most owls live alone, roosting in a tree hollow or tree hole.

Sett: Badgers make their homes underground and keep them very clean. Setts are a maze of tunnels and chambers for sleep and raising their cubs.

Warren: Rabbits make their own homes underground too, in a series of interconnecting tunnels and chambers for sleeping and nesting. Warrens have different entrances so rabbits can make a quick escape.

FIVE WAYS TO BE
A FOREST KEEPER
from Tim Tilley

Number One
Look for signs of seasonal change – birch buds and primroses in spring, foxgloves and poppies in summer. Broadleaved trees change colour in autumn, and lose their leaves in winter.

Number Two
Listen to forest sounds.
Take a family walk during dawn chorus.

Number Three
Learn names; of birds, animals,
flowers, insects, plants and trees.
We care more for what we know.

Number Four
List your local wildlife and let others know.
This important information can help
conservationists protect wild spaces.
 Small actions can make a difference.

Number Five
Love nature and share this with others –
we look after what we love.

CAPTURE THE
MAGIC OF NATURE.

Acknowledgements

Oaks are known to be slow-growing trees, and like an oak, *Harklights* has taken many years to reach maturity. There are many people along the way who are part of its story, and to all I would like to offer heart-felt thanks:

Rachel Lubinski and Jacqui Wakefield, who were there when the story-acorn was first planted, and to Supuck Ruckitan, who inspired me to move the story-sapling to a much-needed bigger pot.

My amazing agent, Julia Churchill for her unwavering support, wisdom and owls. And to Lizza Aiken for founding The Joan Aiken Future Classics Prize. Winning this has changed my world.

My editors Rebecca Hill and Stephanie King for helping *Harklights* grow taller, raising its branches to the stars, and making every sentence shine. Will Steele and Sarah Cronin, for helping me shape the landscape of the book. Sarah Stewart for copy-editing magic, Alice Moloney for proofreading and new insights. Jacob Dow and Katarina Jovanovic for standout publicity and marketing. Everyone at Usborne, for your kindness, support and believing in Wick. He couldn't have found a better home.

The wonderful forest of fellow authors, especially Kiran Millwood Hargrave, Michelle Harrison, MG Leonard, Sophie Anderson, Peter Bunzl, PG Bell, SF Said, Sam Copeland, Darren Simpson, Nizrana Farook and Sophie Kirtley.

My constellation of writer friends and readers for your encouragement and love – Clare Golding, Kat Guenioui, Joanna Barnard, Venetia Maltby, Rosemary Cass Beggs, Sam Lewis, Sara Booth, Rachel Burns, Philippa Neville, Mary Ellen Foley, Richard Fuller, Sally Dickson, Dee Shulman, David Bruce, Col Baird, Sallyanne Sweeney, Duncan McKenzie, Jen Murray, Adebayo Toye,

Alan Findlay, Alison Moulden, Gwen Webber, Lucie Llewellyn, Mark Easton, Miriam Craig, Jez Evans, Jean Owen, Josie McDowell, Kia Mackie, Kate Poels, Hanne Larsson, Janine Yiannakis, Jack Lawrence, Samantha Stacey, Wendy Murphy, Lou Kuenzler, Lorraine Carey, and most especially Chris Williams.

Mum and Dad for support, encouragement and showing me the wonder of nature and stories. The places you took me growing up – the Scottish Highlands, Yosemite, Pembrokeshire and Norfolk – are buried in the corners of my heart. Ben, Andrea and Arlo, for your evergreen love and shining support. Romeo and Anna for everything always, and finding me a night of fireflies to make a childhood wish come true. Andrea, Giulia and Sophia, for summer retreats and days by the lake. Robin Harwood and Jamel Guenioui, for foraging, leaf-hunting and Forest Keeper training.

My grandmother, Joyce Tilley, who lived a life full of courage, and always found friendship in books. *Brendan Chase* was her favourite, and its wild wonder is woven into the roots of *Harklights*. My grandparents, Eric and Vivian Gethyn Jones, and Great Aunt Mollie Coubrough, whose homes were living museums, waiting to be explored.

My forest of family and friends, near and far, for your love and support – Amadei, Tilley, Tilley Loughrey, Toth, Tyson, Amiri, Jenner, Watts, Walters, Wilderspin, Di Nunzio, Gatti, Cini, Peccolo, Flintoft, Fisk, Donovan, Hoffman, Hanauer, Hawthorn, Hommasi, Richardson, Kerrison, Neuls, Monreal-Sayo, Webster, Stockting, Semprebene, Uyama, Brown, Bertotti, Beaton and Baird.

Above all, to Gian Luca, who kindled my ink-dreams, sheltered my strength, and has been by my side every step of this unfolding adventure. To everyone with storyteller hearts – find your voice, tell your story – and to you reader, for sharing in Wick's journey to find a home.